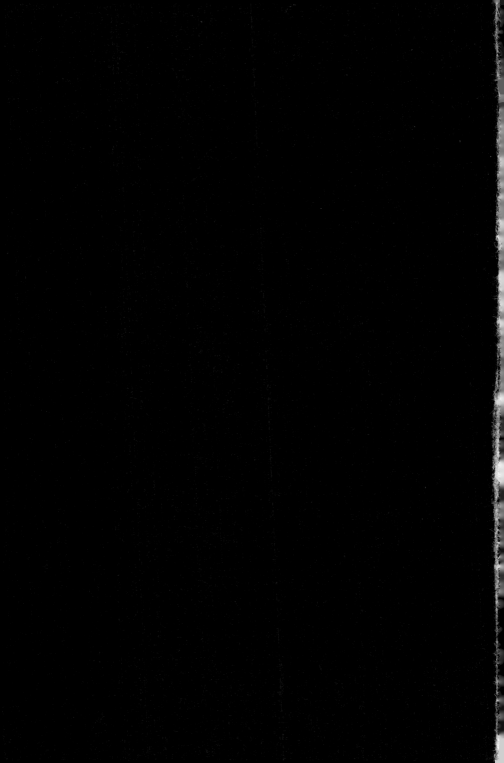

WHITE WIDOW
SECRET SISTERS

TESS SHARPE

Los Angeles · New York

© 2025 MARVEL

All rights reserved. Published by Marvel Press, an imprint of Buena Vista Books, Inc. No part of this book may be reproduced or transmitted in any form or by any means, electronic or mechanical, including photocopying, recording, or by any information storage and retrieval system, without written permission from the publisher. For information address Marvel Press, 7 Hudson Square, New York, New York 10013.

First Edition, September 2025
1st Printing
FAC-004510-25245
Printed in the United States of America

This book is set in Mrs Eaves
Designed by Madison Ackerman

Library of Congress Control Number: 2024951404
ISBN 978-1-368-10199-8
Reinforced binding

Visit www.HyperionTeens.com
and Marvel.com

Logo Applies to Text Stock Only

For the superheroes who changed my life:
Dr. Nick Kongoasa, Steve Fisher, Jim McCarthy,
and the wonderful staff at the
CRRS and Northside Hospital in Atlanta

1.
THE OUTPOST

LOCATION: [REDACTED]

Victor Crane stalks through the hallways of the compound, seething with every step. People scatter when they see him coming, his sour mood clear and the reputation behind it legendary.

He has good reason to be in a terrible temper. Until *she* arrived, his recruits never injured themselves in training like this. But then she swept in a month ago, sent from on high, and he's been left reeling in the wake of her chaos ever since. So far, she's rendered four different girls unconscious during training, made two others cry so hard they hyperventilated, and now this most recent incident.

It's quite enough, if you ask him. She's a terror. A menace. If she hadn't been sent by the Commander himself, he would kick up a much larger fuss about her presence. But now he has real motive to get rid of her. He can't imagine putting up with her for another six weeks as planned. She simply has to go.

He reaches his destination: the holding cell. It takes

a few moments before he's calm and steely enough to enter. He certainly won't be tricked into hyperventilating. Every time he sees her, a ringing starts in his ears. Like his anger at being overruled and defied and shown up has no choice but to pour out in that tinny, annoying sound.

There's something about her that unsettles him. He glances through the tiny window that looks into the cell. The way she's lying on the bench in that cell, whistling to herself like she has no care in the world, is infuriating.

Another deep breath and he unlocks the door, pushing inside with an authority that usually makes the girls quell immediately.

Instead, she continues to whistle. Some jaunty tune he doesn't recognize.

Yelena Belova is not one of the Widows-in-Training under his watchful eye. She comes from the Red Room—the original Red Room. In his world, they call it Headquarters. She calls it home.

Victor vehemently opposed it when Commander Starkovsky suggested an exchange program: Headquarters sends one girl to the Outpost and vice versa. When he was overruled by both Alexander Cady, director of the entire operation, and his own brother, Thomas, it left a bitterness. His twin should be siding with him, not Director Cady. Not only is Victor reluctant to send any of the girls overseas, but he is uneasy at the idea of letting Headquarters get a close-up view into their operation when it has been almost a decade of the Red Room being content with quarterly reports. The sudden interest—and sending their best and brightest—makes him nervous. Did Headquarters want to poach some of the Outpost trainees? Shut down the Outpost operation for good? Or was it truly just a whim of Commander Starkovsky's? To create a sort of girl-spy foreign exchange program for the best of his flock?

"Belova!"

He wants to be the kind of man who can bark an order or a name, but she doesn't even cease her whistling, maddening girl.

Yelena finishes the stanza of the song before finally turning her head to look at him, her blond hair spilling off the edge of the bench with the movement.

There's a streak of blood in it. It's definitely not hers.

She's a savage creature born of violence. He underestimated her when she came here. He thought she was here to learn, but he was quickly disabused of that notion.

No, Belova is here in a move of power from Headquarters, and only he seems to be able to see it. His brother scoffed so hard when he brought it up; he didn't dare voice it to Director Cady.

The Outpost is a fledging organization—they're barely starting their third generation of trainees. Yelena's been cutting a swath through the Duet Generation, and the first generation—the Solo Generation—has fewer than a dozen girls living to show for it.

It's like his brother has forgotten they haven't been wildly successful. But Victor is well aware of their failures. Of the pressure that's been mounting.

"Explain yourself," he says to Yelena.

"I'm whistling to entertain myself," she says flatly. "I thought it was obvious."

"Explain yourself about the incident this morning in the training gym," he says, refusing to play her game.

She slowly rises from the bench. He never would've thought such a small girl could be so deadly, but perhaps that is part of why she was chosen. She's deceptive in size and demeanor. A girl who can slip through the cracks and no one will be the wiser.

"I don't understand," she says.

"Cynthia's leg is broken!"

"That is very sad for her," Yelena says. "But your brother told me to . . . how did he phrase it? 'Give it my all'?"

"He didn't want you put one of the girls out of commission for six months," Victor snarls, ignoring the fact that his brother, Thomas, laughed for a good five minutes over Belova's final move on the sparring mat.

"Your girls have been taught to spar," Yelena comments, her air not just bored, but superior.

That ringing in his ears grows. "Of course they've been taught to spar."

"You don't understand my meaning," Yelena says with the patience of someone speaking to a small child, which is *infuriating*. "Your girls have been taught to *spar*. They have not been taught to fight. Not for their lives. They attack like they don't just expect someone will call things off when it gets too rough—they *know* it. It is a mistake to train them as you have. They do not think with their bodies *and* minds. They keep thinking just with their minds. That gets Widows killed."

"I helped create their training regime!" Victor says, outraged.

"Have you ever had to fight for your life, Commander Crane?" Yelena asks.

Victor knows his silence is an answer because the infuriating girl *smirks*.

"The girls out there . . . soon they will know. Soon it will be their lives. Don't you think it's better that they learn it in here first, where their legs can be fixed and they can grow from the lesson, than out there in the field where they can die from it? Or is this why the commanders back home gossip about the dead Widows of the American Outpost?"

Blood drains out of Victor's face faster than Yelena had broken Cynthia's leg earlier. The sickening crunch that echoed through the sparring room echoes in his ears again, temporarily blocking out the ringing.

"I guess that answers my question," Yelena says, getting to her feet. "Can I go now? It's been hours."

"You're not getting out!"

She rolls her eyes and lies back down on the cot. "Very well." She starts to purse her lips. So help him, if she starts whistling again . . .

"Cynthia's leg is broken in three places!" he bursts out. "That is not what 'giving your all' means."

"Then your brother should have been clearer," Yelena says. "My training did not include such disclaimers as Don't break girls' legs when they go for hidden shivs in a hand-to-hand fight."

Victor flushes. He has been telling himself that knife honed out of a toothbrush handle that clattered to the mat between the girls as they grappled must have belonged to Belova. But if he looks at the situation logically, he knows it couldn't be true. Yelena would've used the crude weapon instead of delivering that brutal blow to Cynthia's leg.

"You're not going to get away with this," Victor tells her. "I'll be writing a report."

"To complain to Headquarters that I am showing how breakable and two-faced your trainees are?" Yelena asks. "After all: It was not my knife, and we both know it."

Victor goes cold. He hasn't thought of it through that lens. He's been focused on Headquarters being outraged that Belova damaged one of their investments and derailed important projects.

"I wouldn't want to reveal such things if it were me," Yelena says. "I would worry it would make me look both incompetent and unable to control my trainees. But what am I but a simple girl."

"You're a Category Five hurricane," Victor says.

"We are accustomed to weathering strong storms in my home, so I'll consider that a compliment," Yelena says. "Are you planning on letting me out anytime soon? So far the only consistently good part of this place is the cafeteria, and Celia told me today was something called Taco Tuesday. I have been encouraged to assimilate into the culture as part of this exchange trip, so I feel like I should participate in this Tuesday ritual of yours."

"You broke Cynthia's leg in three places, and you want *tacos*?"

"As part of my mission to assimilate into your American culture," Yelena says. "And also because I haven't eaten since breakfast, and if I'm to show up for afternoon training—"

"So you can maim another of my girls?"

Yelena's head tilts. "Is it my fault that your girls are trained to spar rather than survive? I don't think it is. I think that's an error in your training methods. If one of the girls back home broke *my* leg, Commander Starkovsky would expect me to learn a lesson from it. And if a girl back home pulled a weapon during an unarmed fight? That girl would not be a Widow anymore. She'd be in a grave. And the girl who disarmed her would get a reward."

The ringing in Victor's ears just grows.

"You want a reward."

"In the form of freedom and tacos, yes. Which I think is a part of this American Dream they speak of?"

"You're—" he starts to say, but before he can finish with *ridiculous*, the door swings open.

"What is this?" his brother, Thomas, asks. "Belova, why are you in here?"

"Your brother put me in here after Cynthia tried to knife me," Yelena says. "Was I supposed to let her stab me, Mr. Crane? Because the Commander would not like that."

"Her leg is broken in three places!"

"Because she tried to stab me with what looked like a

sharpened toothbrush. It was purple and pink, after all."

"Victor, did you actually put her in a time-out?" Thomas asks, his voice mocking.

Blood throbs at his temples. He and his brother used to be in lockstep. But they have always had different interests, and over the years, Thomas's work has put him in closer contact with Director Cady and his secretive ways. His twin now seems content to cut Victor out as the two of them work on secret projects together.

"I still do not see why I'm the one to be scolded," Yelena says. "I gave it my all like I was told. I protected myself when the girl tried to stab me. Again, I ask you: Was I supposed to just let her stab me?"

"No, Yelena," Thomas says. "You did well."

"Thank you," Yelena says, but she doesn't get up; she turns to look at Victor and stares him down, like she's waiting for him to admit defeat.

Only a foolish man admits defeat. And Victor Crane knows he is far from foolish.

XXX

Victor Crane is a very foolish man, Yelena scribbles down in her message to Commander Starkovsky, the man who sent her to America to gather intel on the American Outpost of the Red Room.

Commander Starkovsky has a great deal of scorn for

the American Outpost, and having watched the inner workings of the place for the last few weeks, Yelena can't blame her mentor and handler. There is absolutely cause for his concern. These girls are nothing like the Widows at home. Not the ones in training or the ones who have gone on to glory.

These girls are easily shattered—both their bones and their hearts. Cynthia telegraphed her moves when she reached for her handmade weapon. It was not a bad shiv, Yelena will give the girl that. It could've caused some damage if she didn't see it coming.

While Yelena could blame the girls' temperament or their origins, she suspects it is more due to their training.

The Crane brothers are inefficient and egotistical, and they have little reason to be the latter when they are the former. Commander Starkovsky is already disappointed in the American Outpost—Yelena knows that's the main reason she's here. And he is concerned by the amount of Widows who die in their first years in the field after being trained at the Outpost.

Dr. Thomas Crane seems to be more circumspect than his brother, she continues in her notes. *That is not saying much, but he has the ear and respect of Director Cady the two times I have observed them together. But Director Cady has only been present three times since my stay began, and my ability to get into his office has been hampered so far. He spends much time away from the training center, doing what, I will soon find out.*

Yelena looks up from the small desk tucked in the corner of the room she shares. She can hear footsteps down the hall. She quickly finishes writing: *I will seek out other means to access the Director's office as ordered. I remain, as always, your faithful servant, Commander. —Red Bird*

Folding the note neatly into a small diamond shape, she pockets the now-tiny piece of paper as the door to her room swings open.

2.
THE OUTPOST, DORMITORIES

LOCATION: [REDACTED]
OBJECTIVE: TACOS

Yelena's roommate, Celia, comes bouncing inside the room, her curly hair like a beautiful storm cloud around her head.

"Is it true?" Celia asks excitedly.

"Is what true?"

"That Cynthia tried to knife you in the courtyard and you took her down! Everyone is talking about it."

"Well, everyone is wrong," Yelena says.

"She didn't try to knife you?"

"She did. It was just not in the courtyard. It was during the morning training session. Where were *you* for that?"

"Oh, I had a mission rundown to attend," Celia says with a practiced casualness. "So I was exempt."

"You're going out in the field?" Yelena says, suddenly as curious about Celia's morning as Celia is about Yelena's. She would *kill* to go out into the field right now. While she knows her mission for the Commander is important, she's so *bored*.

"I am," Celia says. "But that's not important! Are you serious? Cynthia actually tried something in *front* of the trainers?"

"In front of Mr. Crane himself. Themselves. What I mean is both of them were there. Victor is very upset with me." Yelena doesn't even bother to try to inject any guilt or shame into her voice. "He locked me up for a while to scold me. He didn't even torture me to get his point across. Not even a little. And then his brother came around and reasoned with him and let me go, so here I am."

"Did you really break Cynthia's leg?" Celia asks.

"I wouldn't have had to go to such extreme measures if she hadn't tried to stab me," Yelena says. "If she had just tried dirty tricks like the others, I would've choked her out like the others. But she had to get creative. And then so did I."

"Yelena, she's going to be *furious*."

"Well, right now, she's going to be sedated. And then she's going to be in an Aircast for months, and I leave in six weeks, so I'm not too worried."

Celia makes a face. "I don't want you to leave! You just got here."

"All good things must come to an end," Yelena says as a bell chimes gently through the halls for lunch. "And speaking of good things, it is taco day, isn't it?"

"Taco Tuesday," Celia says, grabbing her sweater. "I can't believe you've never had one."

"I'm sure you have not had kholodets," Yelena points out as they walk out of their room and into the stream of girls heading to the mess for lunch. She ignores the whispers that follow her and Celia, but it's harder to ignore the way the girls in the hall part like the Red Sea as they pass.

"You're gonna be a legend by the time you leave," Celia mutters.

"Nonsense," Yelena says, even though privately she likes the thought. What else is there to be other than the best? And to be the best, you must do things that etch your deeds into history, like the great Widows who came before her.

Celia pushes the double doors to the mess open. The din inside is at a quiet roar, the sharp voices of girls raised to compete and be the best flying through the air like knives.

"Tell me more about this hot sauce you've mentioned," Yelena says.

"Oh, hot sauce is a must with tacos," Celia says. "There's tons of kinds and flavor profiles. You've got to have some spice with your food, you know?"

"I do not," Yelena says. "But I'm willing to try anything when it comes to food."

"That's what I like about you," Celia says. Her roommate's cheerful demeanor was off-putting to Yelena at the start. She found it strange for a girl trained to be a spy to be so friendly. But she has gotten used to her over the past weeks. Their mutual love for cuisines of all kinds has definitely been helpful. There are times when Celia seems soft, but Yelena witnessed her stepping in to defuse a practice chemical bomb that started to leak once. Everyone knows that while the chemical bombs are practice and will cause no lasting chemical damage or scarring, it doesn't keep the Red Room from filling them with solutions that hurt so badly that some Widows still have nightmares about it, years later. Or so Yelena has heard. Celia pushed the crying girl out of the way and defused the bomb with steady hands and true focus, despite the pain and chemicals eating away at her skin until she resembled a cooked lobster. She saved her entire team from being sprayed with the solution—a true soldier-falling-on-a-grenade moment.

After that, Yelena decided not to underestimate her roommate. Her ability to sacrifice makes her useful, and her cool head and steady hands make her a powerful weapon in the right situations. And there are things you learn about a girl when forced to share a space. Waking to Celia's nightmare sounds is something she's decided to keep to herself, since she likes her.

Nightmares are something that are only whispered about and denied in the Red Room. Yelena is fortunate—she does not wake screaming like some of her sister Widows. But she is not the kind of girl to cry out when she is scared.

She is the kind to lash out. Which is, she supposes, the problem Victor Crane seems to have with her. She can feel him watching from the second-story walkway that loops around most of the rooms in the Outpost. There are always guards and handlers circling in the Red Room, protecting the precious girls. There are so many enemies who would love to get their hands on a Widow, even one in training.

"I'll get the food so you can try a little bit of everything," Celia offers. "You find us a table."

Yelena immediately starts looking for one in a corner. She likes to put walls against her back. But the only table that's in a corner is the one currently being occupied by a lone person she hasn't met yet. She frowns; she was sure that she has met all the trainees at this point. Curious, she draws closer to the table, and the girl looks up before she's even close enough to clock. That tells her at least this one's a bit alive.

"My friend and I need a place to sit," Yelena says. "Can we join you?"

The girl silently moves her bag off the spare chair. Yelena takes it as assent and sits.

"You're the girl from Headquarters."

Yelena nods. "I don't think we've met."

"I've been on a mission," the girl says coolly, like it should impress Yelena.

"Oh my gosh, Johanna, you're back!" Celia sets two trays down on the table, balancing them with an agility that *does* impress Yelena. "Are you two getting to know each other? You should absolutely get along. Yelena, I bet you're the best trainee back home, like Johanna is here."

Yelena's interest in the girl grows with every drip of information she gets. This is the Outpost's best of the best? She thought that was Cynthia, but that girl was too easy to beat. Would this one be any harder?

"*You're* the best?" Johanna asks.

"I think we all know who's *really* top Widow," Yelena says, just as cool as Johanna was a moment ago when mentioning her mission.

"Oh?" Johanna's fingers tighten around her fork like she longs to stab Yelena with it. A fork is a good weapon. Yelena approves. She also doesn't really need a weapon.

"Natasha Romanoff, of course," Yelena continues.

Johanna's fingers loosen around the fork handle.

"The *stories* we've heard about her." Celia sighs. "Anyway, enough shoptalk!"

"Shoptalk?" Yelena asks.

"Work talk," Celia says.

"What else would we talk about?" Yelena asks, just as Johanna says, "What else is there?"

Yelena has enough training *not* to let the smile tug at her mouth. Johanna's temporary smirk tells her that Yelena's the one with superior control. That is useful information to have. She makes a note of it.

"Fine, if we must talk about work: How was the mission, Johanna?" Celia asks.

"Successful," Johanna says.

Celia laughs. "You've got to give me more than that! You're the first in our group to be assigned a solo mission."

"An honor," Yelena says. Johanna's eyes fly up to meet hers as if she can't tell if Yelena is being honest or sarcastic. Yelena decides to let her wonder.

"Did you run into any trouble?"

"It was a simple recon mission, Celia," Johanna says impatiently. "It's not like I was off being a lone assassin."

"I just wanted to know! I'm nervous about tomorrow night," Celia says. "I've only done three group missions," she adds to Yelena. "What's your number?"

"More than three," Yelena says, because she can feel Johanna's gaze burning a hole in her temple.

"Do you think you're better than us?" Johanna asks. "Is that why you won't tell us?"

Yelena refuses to let herself be riled by Johanna.

"From what I have observed the last few weeks here, I am further along in the training than the girls here, as are my sisters back home."

"Wow," Johanna says.

"She *did* break Cynthia's leg," Celia whispers.

"You did *what*?" Johanna says, outrage pulling her eyebrows together into a glower.

"Cynthia made a decision that I suspect she will come to regret but not learn from," Yelena says.

"She came after Yelena with a homemade knife, Johanna! I don't know what she was thinking!"

"A shiv?" Johanna shifts in her seat in a way that perks Yelena's interest and sends her senses clamoring.

"Yeah, one made out of a pink-and-purple toothbrush handle," Yelena says.

Johanna flinches.

"You wouldn't know anything about that, would you?" Yelena asks.

"Of course not," Johanna says, much too quickly to be believed.

"Are you running some sort of black market on toothbrush shivs?" Yelena asks. "Or did she just steal your personal one?"

Red floods Johanna's cheeks at the last question.

"I see," Yelena says. "Don't worry. Your secret is safe with me. And your shiv is now safely locked up in the

Cranes' office. I guess you'll have to make a new one."

"Whatever," Johanna says. "I can't believe you broke her leg."

"I did what I had to not just to survive, but to *win*," Yelena says. Back home, her fellow trainees do anything it takes to reach the top of the leaderboard the Commander makes sure is prominently displayed in their sleeping quarters. These girls seem to share a camaraderie that Yelena has been taught—and knows all too well—can be deadly. *American teamwork culture*, Commander Starkovsky called it scornfully.

Emotions in the field get you killed. Stripping oneself of them is the best way to survive and ensure a glorious return home. No one has taught this crop of girls that, though. Johanna is glaring at her, suddenly distrustful.

"Do you let other people win, even when you see a way out?" Yelena asks. "I thought Celia said you were the best."

Johanna's ears turn red, and she gets up, grabbing her tray. "I'll beat you anytime, Belova. Just name the time and place."

"It was just a question," Yelena says, batting her eyelashes innocently as Johanna storms away. "So touchy," she continues as she looks down at her food.

"She and Cynthia are roommates," Celia says.

"So I've caused a roommate fight by revealing Cynthia stole Johanna's shiv?"

"Probably," Celia says.

"Whoops," Yelena says, so unbothered it makes Celia giggle.

"Okay, we gotta eat before it gets cold! I got three kinds of hot sauce for you to try. Slim pickings around here, unfortunately. But it's something for your first tacos."

Yelena selects the deepest red of the hot sauces, spooning it over the tacos Celia's arranged on the plate. She follows Celia's instructions of sprinkling onion and cilantro over the meat, adding a squeeze of lime at her urging.

"There's chicken, carne asada, and carnitas," Celia says.

Celia watches as Yelena takes her first bite, the spice and burst of lime mixing with the seasoned meat, the fresh bite of onion and the cilantro bringing it all together.

"Well?" Celia asks, but Yelena's mouth's full from her second bite before she can answer. "It doesn't taste like dish soap, does it?" Celia asks, suddenly concerned.

"Dish soap?" Yelena asks when she swallows her second delicious bite.

"Cilantro tastes like dish soap to certain people, the poor things," Celia says.

How strange. Yelena has never heard that. "No, no dish soap. These are delicious."

"I knew you'd like them!"

"The hot sauce brings it all together," Yelena says. After a moment, she adds, between bites, "So, Johanna has a roommate. All the girls have them. But you didn't, when I came here. Why not?"

Celia is quiet for so long, Yelena is not sure how to bridge the silence as it grows and grows.

"I see," Yelena says finally. "You lost her, then?"

Losing girls in training doesn't happen often back home. Of course, once they go out into the world for the Red Room, they don't exactly have a low mortality rate. But when they're trainees, there are supposed to be protocols. They are, after all, precious commodities, as the Commander likes to remind Yelena and her sisters. There seem to be an unusual amount of deaths among the trainees at the Outpost, however. It's one of the things the Commander directed her to question the girls about. By the Commander's count, Georgia Finn, Celia's former roommate, was the sixth girl in the Duet Generation to die *before* completing training. A complete waste of energy, money, and Widow-power.

"Georgia died three months ago on my second group

mission," Celia says in that quick way you say things when you want them to hurt less. "We were . . . we came up together, you know? She shouldn't have gone out that way."

"I'm sorry about your friend," Yelena says. "I will not make you tell me what happened."

She has found that with kind people—and she suspects that Celia is kind at her core—if you state that you aren't going to make them do the thing you want them to do, they often just do it. It is the strangest trick, really.

"It's okay," Celia says, staring at the remains of her tacos. "It's— I don't get to talk about it that much, you know? Everyone just went back to normal."

"The mission is what matters," Yelena says. "I am sure Georgia would've thought the same."

"I know," Celia says. "It's just— Is that the way it always is? Is that the way it is over at Headquarters? You lose a girl and by the next day, her things are cleared from the room and the bed is empty and no one talks about it? It's like she didn't exist."

"We are meant to disappear," Yelena reminds her gently. "To be forgotten."

"But what if I don't want to be?" Celia asks.

Yelena looks down and finds that she has no good answer.

Because the true answer?

Then you're in the wrong place.

⧗

It's like Celia realized she spoke a little too frankly with Yelena during lunch, because she's quiet for the rest of the day, even during dinner, which unfortunately is not a repeat of tacos.

Yelena gives the girl some space. She knows that creeping feeling of dread from having said too much, though she hasn't done such a thing since she was a child. You do it once and you should learn.

But as they settle down for the night, the lights off and the silence stretching, Yelena finds that Celia hasn't learned her lesson.

"Yelena," Celia whispers in the dark. "Are you still awake?"

Yelena almost says no, but she resists the biting urge. "Yes."

"Can I ask you something?"

She surprises herself again and takes the nice route. "Of course." How's that for personal growth?

See, Johanna was wrong. She's not stunted.

So, of course, Celia promptly asks the thing that makes her want to throw all that personal growth out the window, because look at where it gets her.

"Do you remember the before? Before you came to the Red Room?"

Yelena licks suddenly dry lips, staring up at the ceiling in the darkness, wondering how many ways this room is bugged. If Celia is a plant, designed to seek out weak spots. Or worse, if it is just as it seems: that Celia's scared. Maybe she remembers glimpses, like Yelena does. Maybe she yearns for more (not like Yelena, that can't be Yelena, that will *never* be Yelena).

"A little," Yelena says finally, and when Celia lets out a shaky breath she's been holding, waiting for an answer, that tells Yelena exactly what kind of question it was.

"I didn't know if I was crazy," Celia whispers. "The other girls—they acted like they didn't know what I was talking about."

"You should not be asking them. They'll use it against you. Put it from your mind," Yelena says.

"Is that what you do?"

"Yes."

"But aren't you curious? If there's people out there—a family—or—"

"We belong to the Red Room, not to a family," Yelena says firmly. "We are made to fix the problems of the world, but we are not *of* the world. We do not live in it like others do. We are tools to control the world. If given the choice between being an ignorant puppet and being the second hand of the puppeteer, I will choose knowing what the world really is over ignorance of it each time."

Celia's quiet. Too quiet. Yelena feels a flash of something hot and uncomfortable. Something that she barely recognizes but thinks might be guilt.

"It is safer that way," she says, hoping Celia hears the urgency and warning in her voice. "To be a good Widow is to put aside emotion and silly wants in pursuit of a much greater goal."

"I know," Celia says. "You're right. I just—"

"You're not the only one who has the flashes and dreams," Yelena says, almost reluctantly, half out of the desire to quell the strange heat of guilt in her.

"Thank you, Yelena," Celia whispers.

Yelena speaks no more that night, waiting until she hears Celia's breathing soften and steady, burrowed deep in blankets, reassured finally that she is not alone.

She has no comfort of reassurance. She stares at the ceiling and tries not to think of her own moments of *before* that haunt her, but it's impossible after such a conversation.

It's a subject that is barely spoken of back home, just like here. Something that the Outpost has in common with the Red Room, finally.

She knows she was chosen by the Red Room. That is all that they're told, when they wake in those dormitory beds, small and disorientated with a blank slate. She forgets, sometimes, how very young she was when her training started. She does not feel young anymore.

The Red Room taught her about her power and purpose. But with all the knowledge they've instilled in her, they've kept just as much from her. That is the way of power. Others will always have more than her. She finds that does not bother her any.

But the memories do. Can they even be called memories when they're so piecemeal? Nothing is complete in her head; it's just small snatches that almost seem made up.

The warmth of a much bigger hand around her small one. Looking up and seeing a pattern of bright roses on a scarf tied around a woman's head. A wisp of blond hair escaping from the scarf, blowing in the wind as she struggles to keep up on the road. The woman turning back to make sure she's following, but Yelena can't ever get close enough to see her face.

Sometimes Yelena is grateful she can never make out the woman's features.

But sometimes, in her weakest moments, she yearns to know: Are they like hers?

3.
THE OUTPOST, TRAINING ROOM

LOCATION: [REDACTED]
OBJECTIVE: BEAT JOHANNA

"**B**elova, you're up!" Thomas barks across the practice mat. "Parks! On the mat."

Johanna gets up from the bench, strolling to her spot with a gleam in her eyes that sends a warning prickle down Yelena's spine. She wonders if Johanna's taken a page out of her roommate's book and brought another shiv along. Hopefully this one has a better color scheme than the first. Yelena is a fan of black and red, personally.

"Be careful," Celia hisses as Yelena bends down to grab the wraps for her hands. "I heard Johanna trash-talking you before class."

Yelena shoots her a reassuring smile. "Don't worry."

The observation deck that runs along the upper level of the training room creaks as Yelena moves toward the mat. She glances up to see Victor has arrived, watching her every move. She smiles sunnily at him, giving a little bow before she comes to a stop in front of Johanna.

"My brother's been telling me things, Yelena," Thomas says.

"Oh?" Yelena asks innocently.

"He says you think our girls don't know how to fight properly."

"I said they do not know how to survive," Yelena says. "Surviving requires acting like there's no safety net below."

"Well, you're gonna get your wish, Yelena," Thomas says. Yelena glances over her shoulder to see the clock on the wall set to ten minutes. "Cage down," Thomas adds, stepping away from the two girls as the chain-link fighting cage that's suspended from the ceiling slowly descends, enclosing them on the mat.

"Getting nervous?" Johanna asks as Yelena's eyes follow the trainees who move forward to secure the cage bolts to the ground.

Yelena shrugs. "I'm the one who's been trained properly."

"You are so full of it," Johanna says. "Someone needs to teach you a lesson."

"My entire point is that they're teaching the lessons wrong," Yelena says as the final click of the bolts in the ground tells her they're quickly coming to the part where speaking will be an unnecessary waste of air.

Thomas reaches forward and grasps the cage, shaking it back and forth to test its security before stepping back with a satisfied noise. His eyes glitter at Yelena, and she can't tell if he's interested in her winning—or intent on making her lose. She knows which his brother would prefer, but Thomas Crane is more of a mystery to her. He watches her in a different way than his brother. Victor looks at her like she's a nuisance. Thomas looks at her like she's a specimen to be studied under glass.

She thinks she might like Victor Crane's obviousness over his brother's careful scrutiny.

"All right," Thomas says. "You have ten minutes."

"What are the rules?" Johanna asks.

Thomas smiles, a sharp-edged thing that tells Yelena everything she needs to know: She has every reason to be unsettled by this man. She's accidentally challenged him to be cruel, and he's taken hold of that opportunity with a disturbing relish.

"There are no rules, Johanna," he says. "Yelena is right: Survival is what happens when there is no safety net. Just like in the field. No one is coming for you if you fail. Unless it's to hunt you down. It is best my girls learn that . . . starting now."

Johanna squares her shoulders. "I'm ready."

"We'll see," Thomas says, as if he knows exactly how this will play out. Yelena doesn't like that, either.

"Let's begin!" Thomas says. Out of the corner of her eye, Yelena can see the red numbers start to change, but she can't pay them much heed. She needs to move.

She begins to circle as Johanna does the same, the cage around them keeping them from going too far. The girls surround the cage, watching in silence, breathless, to see who makes the first move.

Her hands loose at her sides, Yelena keeps her eyes on Johanna. The girl's a good six inches taller than her, which gives her a certain advantage.

"You're gonna regret talking about how much better you are than all of us yesterday," Johanna says.

"Doubtful," Yelena says, dodging when Johanna lunges forward. The taller girl ends up grabbing air instead of flesh, and Yelena goes low, her leg snapping out and connecting with Johanna's kneecap.

Johanna tries to strangle her scream by gritting her teeth, but it comes out anyway. She reaches forward and Yelena dances out of the way, but Johanna's fingers grasp the end of her ponytail and she *yanks*.

Yelena is down on the floor in a flash, but she manages to recover at the last second, twisting so Johanna doesn't get the full body-whipping movement she'd been hoping for. She isn't going to be dealing with a case of whiplash, thank you very much.

Yelena's hip takes the brunt of the fall and she rolls,

breaking her hair from Johanna's grip. She leaps to her feet, rounding on Johanna with a snarl. Her fist makes contact with the girl's jaw. Johanna's head snaps back, blood and a tooth spraying in an arc out of her mouth. The momentum pins her to the cage and she sags against it, her fingers looping in the chain link as she struggles to stay upright.

Yelena doesn't hesitate or wait for Johanna to recover. She grabs the girl's hair just like Johanna grabbed her ponytail and uses the strands like a rope to swing her head right into the metal pole the chain link is strung around.

She steps out of the way as Johanna slithers to the ground, unconscious and bleeding from the mouth from the previous blow.

"Time!" Thomas Crane says faintly.

"Seventy-eight seconds," a girl with an undercut—Yelena thinks her name is Tiffany—who is manning the clock says. "A new record."

"Goody for me," Yelena says sarcastically, stepping over Johanna and heading over to the cage door. "Can I get out of here now? You might want to send her to the infirmary."

"I'm sure she's fine," Thomas says.

"I'm sure she's not," Victor counters, unlocking the

cage door and brushing past Yelena to check on Johanna. Yelena shrugs and strolls out of the cage to go sit next to Celia.

"She's out cold," Victor announces to his brother. Thomas says something biting to his brother, who shakes his head at first and then nods, raking his hand through his unkempt blond hair.

Victor stalks out of the cage toward Yelena—she is beginning to wonder if that is the only way he knows how to walk: quickly and angrily. She stays seated next to Celia as Victor's brother follows behind at a less angry clip. He's clearly the more rational of these two.

"Do you know what you have done?" Victor demands.

"What you asked: I didn't break any limbs. Mine or Johanna's."

"She's unconscious!"

"She'll wake up eventually," Yelena points out, maybe a bit too smugly because Victor Crane's hand pulls back to slap her or maybe box her ears. It wouldn't be the first time that Yelena's been hit by one of her superiors. She braces for it—even foolish men can deliver a powerful blow—but it doesn't land.

His brother has restrained him, Victor's fist in an iron grip. "Enough," Dr. Thomas Crane says. "Your histrionics are helping no one."

"Johanna's supposed to lead tonight's mission," Victor reminds Thomas. "She can't do that while she's concussed."

"We'll find someone else. The second-in-command."

Next to her, Celia lets out a small, worried groan.

"That would be Celia," Victor says.

Celia's hands knit together in a tangle. Yelena has to bite her tongue to keep from telling her to leave them loose at her sides. Dr. Thomas Crane will read her body language in an instant if Yelena can do it. He is the more intelligent of the brothers, after all.

"Take her to the infirmary," Dr. Crane tells one of the assistant trainers, who nods and snaps at one of the girls to help him load Johanna on a stretcher. Yelena steps out of the way to allow them some space.

"Don't go anywhere," Dr. Crane says, not even looking at Yelena, but pointing in her direction anyway.

"I'm not."

"Celia, you'll have to lead the mission tonight. This is a Priority Red project for Director Cady. It's imperative that we move quickly on the package before it's moved again."

"I understand," Celia says. "But—"

"But what?" Dr. Crane demands.

"But I have not prepared to lead a mission. I've only run two simulations as team leader. And I've never done a field exercise as team leader. I just want to make sure I am the best person to lead a Priority Red project," Celia says. Yelena admires the tricky way Celia weaves her explanation that really boils down to: *I really, really don't want to be in charge.*

"Johanna does have more solo and team leader experience than you," Dr. Crane says, stroking his chin thoughtfully. "I didn't realize you still haven't worked as team leader in a field exercise."

"I am next up as team leader, I believe," Celia says. "I'm sorry I haven't gotten to it in my training."

Dr. Crane shakes his head. "You don't make the schedule, so it's not your fault. But you are unprepared."

"That is my fault," Celia says quickly, even though it really isn't.

"I have a solution to your problem," Yelena says, worried Celia's going to take more blame for things she's not responsible for.

Victor rolls his eyes behind his brother.

"What is that?" Dr. Crane asks.

"I can go in Johanna's place."

"You—absolutely not," Victor says. "You're here to *observe* and train. Not to go out in the field!"

"I have more practical field experience than Johanna," Yelena says. "And since she is the only girl in the Duet Generation who has gone on a solo mission, I seem to have more field experience than all your girls put together. And those are *real* missions. Not field exercises. But I've led at least a dozen field exercises, if that helps."

"She's right," Dr. Crane mutters to Victor, who looks like he's about to grab one of the kettlebells off the weight rack and clobber his brother with it. A sloppy way to die, if you ask Yelena.

"You can't be serious," Victor says. "Director Cady—"

"I will check with him, but I'm sure he'll be fine with it," Dr. Crane says coolly. "It needs to be a team of four. And if we don't move now, Minerva will move the package. Director Cady was very clear: He wants the package destroyed. Belova's been trained by Headquarters. If we give her the mission brief—"

"Don't you dare give her the mission brief!" Victor protests.

Yelena watches the two men argue like it's a tennis match. While she didn't exactly plan on messing up their mission, she isn't going to push away such an opportunity to see some action. Anything to get out of here. She's been so bored. Director Cady is barely ever actually at the training center from what she can tell, which makes spying on him difficult and boring. At least at home there are girls to cage fight who last longer than seventy-eight seconds.

"I'm happy to fill out the quartet, as you need it so badly," Yelena says, bringing a halt to their argument.

"See?" Dr. Crane says.

"Celia is second-in-command," Victor says, flinging his hand dramatically toward Celia. "She should be team leader."

Celia visibly gulps. "I—I will do whatever you ask of me, sir."

Yelena makes a note to teach Celia how to hold in her emotions better. It isn't really about not feeling them. More about putting them in a box somewhere deep so as to not show them. You can open the box later. If you must. Yelena prefers not to, most days . . . weeks . . . months.

"There," Victor says. "It's resolved. Celia will lead the team."

"Celia's team position is about her test scores, not her experience," Thomas says, and they descend into arguing again as Yelena sighs heavily. They'll probably keep arguing until the very last second if someone doesn't stop them.

So she does the only thing she can get away with: She walks right between the two men spitting and spatting like cats over a rotten fish and strolls over to the rack holding the kettlebells, selecting the nine-kilogram weight.

"What are you doing?" Dr. Crane demands.

"I'm going to get a workout in while you argue like petty little men," Yelena says. "I might as well stay warmed up, whatever you decide."

Dr. Crane lets out a bray of laughter that's very donkey-like. But Yelena likes donkeys. Stubborn creatures are ones who survive.

"I will not be embroiled in this!" Victor says. "If something goes wrong, I'll be letting Director Cady know this was your call, Thomas."

"I'm fine with that," Thomas says, pulling out his tablet. "You'll find the mission rundown on your device, Yelena. It's a basic find, retrieve, and destroy. There's a package that's damaging to the Red Room in the Stanley Hotel in New York. There's a special-access penthouse at the top of the hotel where they're keeping it."

"Who are *they*?" Yelena asks.

Dr. Thomas Crane twitches a little, like he didn't expect any questions. "That's not important to your mission. All you need to know is that there will be armed guards protecting the package, and they will be willing to give their lives."

"It's that important?" Yelena asks. "What is it that we're destroying? Files? Weapons?"

Another twitch. "That's not relevant—"

"—to the mission strategy," Yelena finishes for him with a sunny smile. "I understand. You don't need to worry, Dr. Crane. I think quick on my feet, I'll find a shredder or something for the incriminating documents."

"I can neither confirm nor deny there are documents—"

"I know," she interrupts again. More twitching. She probably shouldn't push. His brother would have a vein pulsing in his temple by this point.

"What is our ruse?" she asks.

"You will lead a team of three girls, posing as concert-goers, into the Stanley Hotel. The penthouse is only accessible by a special elevator and code. The elevator code and hotel schematics are in your mission rundown. I advise you go and study them before meeting your team at the armory."

"I understand," Yelena says, excitement surging through her. "I won't let you down, Dr. Crane."

"I hope you don't," the Doctor says. "I do hate it when my brother is right."

Without another word, the man leaves the gym. She wouldn't be surprised if he actually goes and checks on Johanna in the infirmary. How strangely they run things here. Surely Commander Starkovsky has seen the error and rot in it, and that's why he's sent her to observe and report.

Director Cady and the Crane twins have no idea how to raise Widows. But Yelena can help the girls on her team get a taste of the true life they're meant to lead tonight. The thought cheers her. They should get to know what it's really like, instead of being coddled in this strange ivory tower disguised as a red one that Director Cady and the Crane twins have created in America.

She goes directly to her room under Crane's instructions, rooting in her bedside drawer for her tablet. By the time Celia comes back, she is three pages into the mission rundown.

Yelena looks up warily as Celia enters, feeling, for the first time, a flash of alarm when the girl doesn't meet her eyes. It's not like she's never had to deal with a roommate who wants to kill her before—the roommate she had when she was ten was quite memorable, after all—but there's a sudden flash of guilt in her gut. She didn't even consider if Celia might have *wanted* to lead the team.

"Are you all right?" Yelena asks.

"Yeah," Celia says, in a way that distinctly tells Yelena: *No, I'm not*. She fusses with the clothes in the top of her chest of drawers, keeping her back to Yelena.

Yelena tries to take the hint and turns back to her tablet, but Celia keeps closing and opening drawers in such a distracting way that it's difficult.

"Is there something you wanted to talk to me about?"

she asks, trying to keep her voice level and polite even though she is neither.

"Yes," Celia says, with such a sharp hiss on the *s* it sends a tingle down Yelena's spine. Maybe she was wrong when she assessed Celia as an intellectual threat but not a physical one. "Why did you do that?"

"Do what?"

Celia rolls her eyes like Yelena is playing dumb, and while that can be useful, she's not this time. "Why did you volunteer like that?"

Yelena shrugs. "It seemed like the thing to do. He was going on and on about how they needed four girls." She glances down at the rundown on her tablet. "Unless the package is a three-headed dog or something, I'm not sure why there needs to be four girls."

"This mission is gnarly," Celia says. "At least that's what everyone's been whispering. And you didn't really answer my question."

Yelena's head tilts as she thinks through her angles here. "Are you angry I volunteered?"

Celia shakes her head and crosses her arms. She's shaking a little. That's when it dawns on Yelena: Celia's not angry that the burden of team leader hasn't fallen to her. She's *relieved*. And she's worried Yelena will think of her as weak because of it.

"Were you scared to be in charge?" Yelena asks.

Red floods across Celia's cheeks and the bridge of her nose. She doesn't confirm it, but the silence hangs heavy between them.

"It's not that I don't want to get out there," Celia whispers. "It's just that I don't think I'm ready to lead yet."

Yelena nods, and Celia fidgets in the quiet between them before she finally breaks it: "Do you think I'm a coward, Yelena?"

Yelena shakes her head. "I think you're wise," she says. "Not smart. Wise. There's a difference, I've found. A smart person would take the lead, even if they weren't prepared. A wise person considers the consequences, not just the benefits. To put your ego aside to look after the greater good of the mission is to be a true Widow. We are not made for ego. We are made for the mission. For the Red Room. Nothing else."

"Nothing else," Celia echoes, but she makes it sound sad. Yelena has never thought of it that way until now. She shakes the thought and feeling off, tucking that little box inside her, not to be examined too closely.

A clear head, strong fists, and a loyal heart, she reminds herself. That's what she'll need tonight.

4.
THE OUTPOST, ARMORY

LOCATION: [REDACTED]
OBJECTIVE: PREPARE FOR MISSION

"**H**ave you ever been to a concert?" Celia asks as they head down to the armory. "Like, undercover or something?"

Sometimes, late at night, when she's too tired to drive away the thoughts, Yelena remembers snatches of music. Clapping hands. The feeling of joy that only comes from a gathering. She can never venture deep into the memory, even if she wanted to. It cuts off whenever she tries. So she's stopped trying. Yet still, in the quiet moments of the night, it comes.

"Not yet," Yelena says. "But one of the girls back home, she worked as a decoy at the opera for a whole season. She got to wear the prettiest dresses. But her hair could've been better. Not that I would've said that to her face."

"Oh yes you would have," Celia says, laughing as she holds the door to the armory open. The other girls are already inside.

Yelena grins slyly as she steps inside. "All right, maybe

I gave her some pointers later on. She was wearing it all slicked back—it didn't suit her sweet face. She needed some"—she waves her hands near her own cheeks—"fluff around her cheeks, you know?"

"Layers make everything come together," Crystal says, nodding sagely and brushing her hand through her own perfectly layered hair.

"Good, we're all here," Victor Crane says. "We're running a little behind and there's traffic, so let's get started. Here's how it'll go, trainees. International pop star Kaylie Quick will be in New York tonight for a big concert on her world tour, providing the perfect cover for your mission. You will blend in with the crowd leaving the concert—the hotel is right next to the amphitheater. The streets and hotel will be full of teenage girls going on and on about love and *empowerment*." He makes it sound like a dirty word. "All you need to do is blend in with the regular girls and get to the private elevator. The package will be guarded upstairs as well, so Bex, our tech expert, is here to equip you with the appropriate weaponry."

"Afternoon, Widows," says Bex, a short woman in her early twenties with hair cropped close to her head and elfin features. "I've got some fun toys for you today." She presses a button, and shutters roll up on the walls, exposing weaponry of all kinds. Some Yelena recognizes—what girl doesn't desire a sharp knife, just in case?—but others puzzle her. Are those . . . cat-ear headbands? Surely not.

"As you'll be posing as normal teen girls returning from a night out, we've had to get kind of creative," Bex explains. "I've got your Widow's Bite bracelets here." She points to the right wall.

"They're all awkward," Yelena says, drawing forward to pluck one off the wall. It looks more like a watch than a weapon meant to render even the strongest person unconscious.

"Careful, Yelena!" Bex warns as Yelena prods the bracelet. But it doesn't shock her when she pokes at it—it lights up in a dizzying array of colors.

Yelena raises her eyebrow at it. "Terrifying," she says.

"It is when properly activated," Bex says, coming over and flipping the bracelet upside down, tapping the bottom three times. "There you go, my impatient Widow."

"I'm not—" Yelena protests.

"Oh yes you are," Bex says. "I know your type. You love the field so much you can't wait to get in it. But learning the proper way to handle the equipment is important. So step back and don't touch anything without my permission. If you had picked up the headband wrong, you could've sliced your fingers off."

"Really?" Yelena's eyes spark in interest, flying to the cat-ear headband immediately.

Bex grins. "Definitely," she says. "And it's perfectly balanced for throwing. It's like a death Frisbee."

Yelena's hooked. She steps back to let Bex finish.

"We've got the headband," Bex says, raising her voice as she plucks the headband from the wall. "This thing is razor-sharp, everyone. Handle with care. Your bracelets will also fry any digital lock you come across."

"Or someone's brains," Yelena mutters.

"That, too," Bex agrees. "Moving on to toiletries. We've got the classics: knockout perfume, mints that will make anyone vomit five seconds after the mint dissolves, a tube of lipstick that's actually a paralytic dart, a compact full of cementing solution instead of face powder—just add water. I've also got acid gum, and the strings of friendship bracelets you've all been given can be unwrapped into a weight-bearing rope. Or, I suppose, a garrote."

"These flimsy things?" Celia asks, plucking at the stack of friendship bracelets on her wrists.

"They're not made with regular elastic," Bex says.

"So cool," Crystal says.

"Anything else?" Victor asks Bex.

"I just need everyone to take their radios," Bex says, pulling out a slim box from her pocket. "These hook around your back molar," she explains, flipping open the box and letting the girls each select one.

"Ew," Tiffany says, but she takes the radio and shoves it in her mouth after Bex demonstrates.

Yelena places her own radio before she follows Celia as the girls line up to receive their weaponry disguised as concert gear. The little plastic backpacks seem so silly—dangerous things can hide in plain sight. But Yelena fills hers up with the gear provided, pulling on and securing the cat-ear headband behind her ears.

"How do I look?" she asks Celia, half dreading the answer.

"Like a very grumpy kitty cat," Celia says, laughing. Meanwhile, she's absolutely pulling off the cat ears. In fact, she looks completely at home dolled up like a normal girl, aglow with the excitement of her first night out on the town.

It's either a good act, or . . .

Yelena tries not to think about the alternative: that Celia actually yearns to be a normal girl. She doesn't even want to think it into existence because that path leads to nothing good.

Yelena slides a second Widow's Bite bracelet onto her wrist. She wishes the weight of them was familiar and comforting, but these are so much bulkier than the ones at home. She misses her sleek bracelets and simple black uniform. She's never had to dress up for a mission before. Commander Starkovsky always says she is much more suited for ambush missions than undercover ones.

This mission is about deception and a certain kind of stealth. Because no one ever pays little girls any mind, do they? There's a magic to it, the way that adults overlook girls. Especially if they're all pink and glittery and in love with something everyone likes to scorn because it makes them feel better. Higher.

Celia carefully arranges her cat-ear headband around the golden butterfly clips already in her hair. "I'm so nervous," she whispers to Yelena. "It feels like my heart's going to beat out of my chest."

"Deep breaths on the transport over," Yelena directs as Victor shouts, "All right, girls, you've got a minute left to prepare. Then we're heading over to the loading dock. Remember: Director Cady's order is to find and then eliminate the package. You do not leave the penthouse until the package is eliminated. Do you understand?"

"Yes, sir!" they all shout as he marches out of the armory like he's heading off to war himself. Yelena rolls her eyes as she follows. That man would crumple into a fetal position and cry if he were actually in a fistfight, let alone a war.

"Let's head down to the transport," Yelena says, infusing her voice with as much authority as she can. Being a leader doesn't just mean being an example, it means watching out for everyone. Sacrificing yourself for the better of the team and mission, if need be. She understands why Celia would feel worried about assuming such a role, but Yelena feels something entirely different: excitement. It's like fuel to her fire, the idea of being in charge, plunging into a new mission where the objective is the only thing she has to focus on.

The girls follow her in a line. Yelena tries not to think that she looks a little silly—her glittery skirt may have a convenient hidden pocket for her paralytic-dart lipstick, but it softly jangles with each movement, a whisper of sequins stirring the air. She doesn't like how much noise she's making. Stealth is a Widow's best weapon. And glittery skirts *reflect* light instead of absorbing it.

She misses her catsuits. Those are bulletproof, too.

The van awaits them in the underground parking lot. The girls board, and Crystal closes the sliding door and settles into a seat next to Tiffany, across from Celia and Yelena.

"Buckle up," Celia directs them as they pull out.

"Such a Goody Two-shoes," Tiffany says, but she fastens her seat belt.

"Yes, how strange that I don't want us to die in a car accident before our *very first mission*," Celia says. "Would you prefer a gun with no safety, Tiff?"

"If it makes me shoot faster, sure." Tiffany shrugs.

"Or you could just practice and get better," Yelena says. "I've seen you at the shooting range. You have miles to go."

Crystal snickers as Celia ducks her head to conceal her smile.

"I may not be the strongest markswoman," Tiffany says. "But hand to hand, no one can stop me. If I'd been in that cage with you, Yelena, you'd be the one in the infirmary right now."

"Big words," Yelena says. "Maybe we'll see some action tonight and you'll be able to back them up."

"Here's to hoping," Tiffany says.

"Does anyone know *what* the package is?" Crystal asks.

"It doesn't say in the mission brief," Tiffany says. "We'll have to wing it, whatever it is."

"Why do you think we can't know?" Crystal persists.

"It doesn't matter," Yelena says firmly.

"How are we going to know where it is in the penthouse?"

"She does have a point there," Celia says.

"We'll figure it out," Yelena says. "The brief says the package is located in the secondary bedroom. If it's not obvious what it is, we'll set the place on fire."

"Yelena, we can't just resort to arson like that," Celia says. "There's an entire hotel's worth of people at the Stanley. What if we set the entire place on fire?"

"Fine. Arson is a last resort," Yelena agrees, settling back. "I suggest we all rest or go over the notes. It's a few hours' drive into the city." She thought it strange they had to take a van, but apparently the airspace above the concert is restricted. If they used even one of the stealth copters, it might attract too much attention.

She tilts her head against the seat, closing her eyes.

"How can she rest at a time like this?" she hears Crystal hiss to Tiffany, but there's no answer.

Yelena keeps herself from smiling. In her head, she can see the blueprint of the penthouse that accompanied the mission debrief. She traces the entrance from the elevator . . . down the hall, into the sitting area lined with windows, then up the stairs, and thirty feet to the right is her target.

Sixty seconds or less, she tells herself. That's how long it would take with no guards blocking her.

The van rumbles toward the city as Yelena plots and the girls chatter around her.

"Has anyone . . . actually been to a concert?" Crystal asks.

"Oh my god, Crystal," Tiffany groans.

"What? I'm just trying to get in the zone. I listened to the entire set list and everything. I think I like the song 'Red Scarf' the best. See, I wrote the lyrics on my arm like the other girls do." She pulls up her sleeve slightly to show the lyrics in eyeliner written down her arm.

"There's nothing wrong with doing your homework," Celia says. "My favorite song was 'April.' It was so emotional!" She sighs. "Love triangles seem complicated."

"We're not getting quizzed about the concert, we're just using it as cover for why we're in the hotel. Do you really think the doormen or the security guards are gonna be like, *Name ten Kaylie Quick songs or we won't let you pass*?" Tiffany asks incredulously.

"I'm trying to get into character," Crystal says. "Just because you have no artifice in you and you're more like a bludgeon doesn't mean I have to— Ow! Don't you dare kick me, Tiffany!"

"Don't be a baby."

"I was just telling the truth! You always look like you're ready to punch someone at all times. You're never going to be able to go undercover on your own. You're only good in a group, Tiff. And you know what happens to Widows who can't work solo."

"I will hurt you," Tiffany says. Yelena's eyes open just in time to see Tiffany ripping her headband off to go for Crystal.

"Hey!" Yelena unbuckles her seat belt and scrambles to put herself between the two girls. "Stop that," she says, staring Tiffany down. "Don't make me put you down like I did Johanna," she adds, even though she's quite sure that if she knocks Tiffany or Crystal—or both of them—unconscious, the Crane brothers will unite in their fury toward her in some sort of supercharged twin way. "I understand if you two have some nerves you want to work out. But we don't do that by attacking our teammates. We need each other to destroy the package."

"Then tell her to stop needling me," Tiffany says.

"Maybe wipe off your *I'm gonna punch a girl* face and *smile* once in a while," Crystal says.

"That's it." Tiffany lunges for her.

"No!" Yelena yanks the girl into the seat. Tiffany tries to rear against Yelena's hands as they press her shoulders into the vinyl, but her eyes grow wide when she realizes she's not able to move.

"I am your leader," Yelena says. "You will sit. You will stay."

"Like a dog," Crystal says mockingly.

"*You* will shut up," Yelena says to her over her shoulder. "If we don't work together, we're in trouble. So put your issues aside right now. Or I'll toss you all out of the van and go do the mission myself."

Celia laughs. "I'll help."

"You'd never," Crystal says.

"Try me," Yelena threatens.

Crystal falls silent. Tiffany shifts uncomfortably across from her.

Yelena keeps her face cool, calm, and collected. Smooth, like a still pond in the morning.

"Fine, we'll get along," Tiffany says reluctantly.

"Or else," Yelena says.

"Or else," Crystal agrees begrudgingly.

5.
THE STANLEY HOTEL

LOCATION: NEW YORK CITY
OBJECTIVE: FIND THE PACKAGE AND DESTROY IT

The stream of concertgoers heading down the streets is overwhelming. Fans of all kinds, jamming them from all sides. Yelena takes a deep breath as they blend in with the crowds heading down the sidewalk. Yelena nods to Celia as they pass the café that will be their rendezvous point later. Hopefully they won't get separated, but just in case, they know where to find each other.

"Wasn't the concert great?" some girl chirps behind her. "I cried so much during 'Red Scarf.' Kaylie Quick is a genius. Can you believe she sang the eight-minute version?"

"It was incredible," says another girl, and they push ahead of Yelena, arms linked, their friendship bracelets clinking with each step.

"There's the hotel," Crystal says, nudging Yelena as they turn the corner and the Stanley comes into sight.

"Check your radios," Yelena says, touching the left side of her jaw slightly. There's a sharp little buzz in the back of her mouth, signaling the radio is activated. "All good?"

"All good," they chorus. She can hear them next to her, but also in her head. It's a feeling that always takes a few minutes to get used to.

"Let's go. Remember: We destroy the package no matter what."

Yelena puts herself in front, crossing the street toward the Stanley Hotel, her teammates trailing after her, looking like any other girls who just had the best night of their lives. The blue-uniformed bellboy opens the door for them as they approach, and Celia links arms with Yelena like the girls in the street did. It's nice, like they are real friends instead of pretend.

The lobby is all marble columns and velvet furniture that must be a pain to keep clean. The elevators are tucked away in a corner, enormous palm fronds blocking the golden doors from full view.

"Split up for recon," Yelena mutters.

Celia lets go of her and heads to the right, positioning herself at the marble column, bending to fuss with the intricate straps on her sparkly boots. The placement gives her the perfect view to see whoever's coming toward the lobby—and past the elevators.

Tiffany goes to the left, tucking herself behind one of the palm trees. Crystal takes the seating area, perching on one of the velvet armchairs while Yelena walks toward the elevators, digging through her see-through backpack for her perfume as she stands behind a group of people who are milling around the first three elevators, waiting for them to bring them up to their rooms.

She turns her head to the left, where a man in a suit and sunglasses stands next to the fourth elevator, his hands folded in front of him, every line of his body screaming *Back off*.

"Someone call me back to the lobby," she says softly into the radio.

"Hey! Hey! There you are!"

Celia pops out of nowhere, skipping over to Yelena, curls bouncing. "I thought I lost you! Come on, we're gonna get snacks before we go up to the room."

She pulls Yelena back into the lobby, where they both lean against one of the columns, subtly watching the steady stream of people heading in and out of the elevators.

No one even tries to go for the fourth elevator.

"The mission brief didn't say the elevator was guarded, just that we'd need a code to get to the penthouse," Celia says.

"I know," Yelena says, trying not to stare too obviously at the elevator's guard. There's a bulge at his shoulder that tells her he's packing some serious weaponry. "We need a different approach," she says. "We can't just attack him. The lobby's too crowded."

"What about a distraction?" Tiffany suggests over the radio. "One of us draws him away, the others get in the elevator?"

"He won't leave his post," Yelena says. "I can tell. Violence would be the only way to get him away from the doors. Unless . . ."

She watches as the stream of people go in and out of the other elevators, an idea sparking in her head.

"Head to the elevators," she tells the girls. "We're going to access the penthouse a different way."

"How?" Crystal asks as Yelena and Celia begin to move back toward the elevators.

"Follow my lead," Yelena says. The four of them wait behind another group of girls, who crowd into the empty elevator.

"We'll take the next one," Yelena calls, and the doors swish closed, leaving just them and the guard in front of the row of elevators. The lobby hums behind them and Yelena considers it for a split second: just attacking him.

But she breathes deep and reminds herself that subtlety is an art. When the elevator closest to the guarded one lights up and then dings, Yelena strides forward, her teammates following.

"What are we doing?" Crystal hisses as the doors close and Yelena presses 14.

"Make a cradle with your hands," she directs Celia and Crystal. "Boost me up." She gestures to the top of the elevator, where an emergency hatch is set.

"You're going to access the other elevator from the shaft?" Tiffany asks, cluing in instantly. She's smart, Yelena will give her that. "That's brilliant!"

Tiffany presses the emergency stop on the elevator, and they shudder to a halt as Celia and Crystal boost Yelena up to access the emergency hatch. It's a tight fit, but she squeezes through. Next to her, the elevator to her left begins its descent from the upper floors. Yelena tilts her head up, her heart rate climbing as she sees how high the cables run. It's a cavernous space where every movement echoes.

Moving in a crouch, she gets over to the edge of her elevator, looking down. It's a big drop, but hopefully she won't break anything.

"I'll meet you on the fourteenth floor," she says into her radio before flipping off the edge of the regular elevator, then landing with a graceful roll on the penthouse elevator. The momentum carries her to the very edge of the steel box, and she winces at the way the thump shakes the elevator. She stays frozen, worried the guard will have heard something.

The elevator carrying her friends begins its climb to the fourteenth floor. Yelena has to get to work. She crawls along to the top of the penthouse elevator, searching for the edge of the hatch. Her fingers find it and she's just about to start to pry it open when the steel under her shudders and they begin to move.

Someone's inside the penthouse elevator. Yelena tilts her head up. She has exactly nineteen floors until she gets squished.

Make that eighteen.

"Someone's in the elevator," she whispers into the radio.

"What?" Celia's voice crackles in her ear.

"What do we do?" Tiffany demands.

"I won't be making it to the fourteenth floor. I need to get into the elevator and overpower whoever's in it and I'll need to time it right, which means I'll need to take a straight shot to the penthouse. This may be the only chance one of us has to get to the package. Get back to the lobby. If you can, find another way up to the penthouse. I'll send the elevator back down."

"But how?" Crystal asks.

"Figure it out!" Yelena hisses, tapping the side of her jaw that the radio's hooked to, turning it off. She doesn't need Crystal in her ear when what was a team mission has suddenly turned solo.

She pulls the emergency hatch open as the elevator continues its ascent, the point of no return getting closer and closer with each breath. Peering inside, she sees the guard from the lobby. They must switch shifts or something.

He's standing close to the door, which means when she drops silently into the elevator behind him, he doesn't even turn.

Yelena unwinds the string of friendship bracelets around her wrist, twisting them in her hands. Two steps and a quick sweeping movement. The guard's first indication someone's in the elevator with him is the clink of beads that spell out *the love of my life is me* . . . right before those very beads are suddenly cutting into his skin, the string holding them together titanium strong.

He fights the friendship-bracelet garrote as it begins to cut off his air supply. He's stronger than Yelena, but when he stops fighting the strangulation and goes for his weapon, she *twists* the bracelet-garrote, bringing her target closer. The electric crackle of her Widow's Bite fills the air as it knocks him to the ground, unconscious.

Panting, she unwinds the garrote from his neck, the strands of beads trailing after her as she bends down, pulling the gun out of his jacket. It's made for electronic bullets—ones designed to send shock waves through the body, much like her Widow's Bite bracelets. But it's better than nothing. She straightens as the elevator dings, gun in one hand, friendship-bracelet garrote in the other, razor-sharp cat-ear headband firmly tucked behind her ears.

She may have expected her team to be with her when locating and destroying the package, but she's a Widow.

The doors slide open.

She's ready for anything.

6.
THE STANLEY HOTEL, PENTHOUSE

LOCATION: NEW YORK CITY
OBJECTIVE: FIND THE PACKAGE AND DESTROY IT

The penthouse is dark and quiet. There's something instantly foreboding about it—how the glass reflects all the chrome staircases and makes it hard to see where the rooms end. A fun-house effect, warping reality.

It makes her want to shiver.

Yelena presses *1* on the elevator's panel to send it back down to the lobby before she steps out. Maybe her teammates will find a way up, but she's not counting on it.

It may just be her now. But a Widow always gets the job done.

She moves swiftly, as silent as a shadow, hugging the wall as she heads to the living room. It looks like the bedrooms are upstairs, which means the package is on the second level.

The flicker out of the corner of her eye is the only warning she has before the man is on her. As she goes down, she jerks her elbow back and hits something soft. His gun goes clattering to the ground, skidding under one of the couches.

Yelena twists in his hold, his arm like an iron bar against her chest, pinning her arms.

She wiggles her leg out from under him, hooking her calf around his and using the leverage to flip them. Her arms free, she slips her hand in her skirt's hidden pocket, pressing the bubblegum-pink lipstick against his neck and twisting the bottom of the lipstick to release the dart.

He lets out a startled grunt at the sting of the dart, his hand coming up to slap the spot.

His hand freezes there and Yelena pushes off him, scanning the area warily. Just two guards when the Outpost sent a whole team of girls? There should be more men for such a desirable item, whatever it is.

That feeling of something not being quite right weaves through her like a snake in tall grass as she makes her way upstairs, the paralytic lipstick tucked in her palm, the friendship bracelet garrote wrapped around her free hand.

When she reaches the second floor, Yelena moves swiftly down the hall, focused on the light shining through the crack of the first door. Maybe *this* is where the rest of the guards are.

Flattening herself against the wall, she peers through the gap, trying to get a good view into the room.

No guards. Just a woman sitting in a tufted leather

chair near the window, her blond hair pulled up into a French twist, her oversize oatmeal-colored sweater falling off one of her shoulders as she knits and hums, oblivious to the fact that both her guards have been taken out.

Yelena weighs her options: the positives and negatives of bursting into the room and taking the woman by surprise or using stealth. She can't see the package, which means she might need answers from the woman before she knocks her out, so she keeps the lipstick at the ready but tucks the friendship bracelets back into her pocket. With her free hand, she pulls off her cat-ear headband and twists it into its lethal shape, the sharp edge of the blade exposed with her simple movement, as a plan begins to form in her head.

These are the moments she lives for, when the world narrows down to her heartbeat and the mission and everything is clear like glass and sparkling like snow frozen crisp overnight.

This is what she was trained for.

This is what she was *made* for.

She slips into the penthouse bedroom, the door not even whispering a noise as she pushes it open. There's a reason they learn ballet in the Red Room—it requires grace and flexibility and gives you the ability to skim and float across the floor, soft-footed and silent. She comes up on the woman from behind, her makeshift blade pressing against the woman's throat before she's even aware someone's in the room.

The woman's breath hitches against the thin blade, and it skims over her skin. Blood wells and drops onto the knitting in her lap.

"Don't move," Yelena says. "Tell me where the package is."

"I don't know what you're talking about."

"I don't like to play games," Yelena says. "I'm here for straightforward answers." She presses the headband against the woman's throat just a little. A straightforward threat. She is a girl of her word, after all. "So let's try again: Where is the package?"

She can see the woman's face in the reflection of the window. She has a sweet face, an innocent face. But Yelena knows looks can be deceiving. She's a perfect example of that.

"I don't—" For the first time, the woman's eyes catch on the reflection of the scene they make in the window. She lets out a startled gasp, scraping the headband turned knife against her skin farther. "Oh my god!"

"Answer me," Yelena says.

"Oh my god!" the woman says again, staring at Yelena, and she jerks *into* the lethally sharp headband, so hard that Yelena has to yank it away before she accidentally cuts the woman badly and ruins her whole line of questioning.

The woman takes advantage of the freedom to scramble to her feet, but instead of trying to run or attack, she just whirls around and *stares*.

"You're— It's you. It's *you*," the woman stutters out, almost like she's seen a ghost or something. Yelena's skin prickles like stinging ice, discomfort raging through her. Who is this woman? She's acting like she knows her, and Yelena has never seen her in her life.

"What are you doing here?" the woman demands. "Did they send you? Why would they send *you*?"

"Where is the package?" Yelena asks again, trying to infuse as much strength into it as possible. She shouldn't have backed her target against the window. She could flee out the balcony.

But she keeps her feet planted, even as her shock at seeing Yelena starts to fade. Her eyes skitter to the right. Yelena's follow—landing on the door that leads to the adjoining bedroom. She feints toward the right. The woman cries out, jerking forward, her knitting needles raised, still attached to the fuzzy purple mohair monstrosity she was working on.

Yelena dodges the needles—what in the world is with her and almost getting stabbed by not-knives lately—and grabs the yarn and *yanks* with a spinning movement, forcing the momentum down. Her foe doesn't have time to let go, her fingers tangled in the yarn, and she's jerked onto the ground by the force of Yelena's spin. Stunned, she lies there on her side, gasping for breath as Yelena rolls into a kneeling position and pulls out the paralytic.

"No," the woman moans.

"Be glad it's not a bullet," Yelena says.

The woman tries to grab her wrist weakly.

"What are you doing here?" she asks again, a broken thread of confusion in her voice. "Are you here to save her?"

Yelena jabs the paralytic into the woman's neck. She jerks, trying to fight it, before the drug sets in.

Yelena hurries toward the door, yanking it open. It's another bedroom, smaller. A bed, a desk, an armoire instead of a closet.

Are you here to save her?

The question rings in Yelena's ears as she takes the steps toward the armoire, counting in her head. One step. Two. Three. Four. Five. Six.

Why didn't the Cranes tell her this was an assassination mission?

Destroy the package.

This is Victor Crane's way of getting back at her. She sees that now. He thinks she doesn't have it in her. Or he thinks she'll fail without all the facts. Without even the correct mission directive.

What an imbecile. Well, she'll prove him wrong. She'll

show him exactly what kind of Widow she is. What kind of Widow Headquarters is creating compared to his weak little girls at the Outpost who cry when their bones break.

She'll destroy the package and dump the body on the doorstep of Crane's office herself.

The thought fixed in her mind, her triumph and anger rising, Yelena jerks open the armoire door.

For a moment, it hangs there—that feeling of anticipation before the fall.

And then she's diving off a cliff, a stomach drop of a feeling as the ground hurtles closer and the crash is inevitable.

There's a little girl crammed in the corner of the armoire, her knees held to her chest, her head tucked into them. When the light falls into the space, she raises her head.

Yelena sees her face.

Yelena sees *her* face. *Yelena's* face. Her mind can't wrap around it for a moment as she stares down at a girl who has her face from when she was a child, round cheeked and straggly haired.

Her eight-year-old self stares right back at her—a perfect replica—though this girl is red-eyed and squinty and tear-streaked in a way she never was at that age, thank you very much.

"Who are you?" the girl with her face asks.

7.
THE STANLEY HOTEL, PENTHOUSE

LOCATION: NEW YORK CITY
OBJECTIVE: DESTROY THE PACKAGE

Yelena opens her mouth—to scream, to yell, to demand . . . what? Answers? What are the answers when confronted with something like this? What are the questions?

But before she can even find any words, there's a boom below.

The door to the elevator in the foyer blasts open. The girl flinches into Yelena's hold instead of away in reaction to the noise, and she is so small in her arms. So breakable.

But Yelena's supposed to break her. She's supposed to snuff her out. To kill her. Those are the orders. That was the mission. Snap her neck, throw her off the balcony, slit her throat, they're all options.

She's capable of all of them, isn't she? They made her capable, a weapon.

Her hands aren't moving except to draw the girl tighter to her chest.

"Looks like she made it up here," Yelena hears someone—she thinks it might be Tiffany—say in the foyer.

They're walking past the guard Yelena disarmed. They'll send someone up here to secure the room while the rest spread through the penthouse. They'll see the package. They'll understand what the mission really is.

They will not hesitate.

Why is she hesitating?

The girl with her face lunges forward, trying to duck under Yelena's arm. She catches her elbow at the last second, yanking her back.

"Shhh!" She claps a hand over the girl's mouth, holding her tight. "They'll hear you."

Why is she warning her? Why isn't she snapping the girl's neck?

Why won't her hands work? Yelena's body does not feel like it's hers. Or maybe it's the opposite.

Maybe her body never belonged to her until now. Maybe it was theirs. The Red Room's.

And now . . . it's hers?

She shakes the thought away as she clutches the girl tight and listens.

"Looks like she got them all," Yelena hears downstairs, accompanied by the crunch of boots on broken glass from the mirror she'd thrown the second guard against before heading upstairs.

Why isn't she calling out? Why isn't she telling them *All clear*?

Move your damn mouth, Belova!

Her hands dig into the little girl's shoulder. Her mind spins, desperately trying to grasp sanity, understanding.

A sister? Is this what the girl is? Is her long-forgotten mother here in America and she had another daughter? That must be it. That *must* be it.

But why would the Crane brothers want a sister dead?

The girl tilts her head, looking toward Yelena. She seems to be searching for something—does she know? Does she recognize Yelena? Does she understand something Yelena does not?

"Where's your pendant?" the girl hisses. "Show it to me!"

Yelena doesn't have time to puzzle through the question because . . .

Tap, tap, tap.

Footsteps up the metal staircase.

Destroy the package. That is the mission.

The girl's pulse thrums in the crook of her elbow where Yelena's gripping her. Or is that Yelena's heart that's beating so fast, bleeding into the girl's skin?

The child wrenches in Yelena's hold, turning to face her. Her eyes go wide as they settle on Yelena's collarbone, where a glow-in-the-dark necklace is still looped. "You're not wearing the pendant. You're not one of them!"

It's fascinating, seeing the realization and thought

process play across her own younger features. An outside, bizarre experience of hindsight. Like watching a video of yourself lying as a child, all the experience of the years allowing you to pick out the childhood tells.

The girl tries to yank free, but the tap, tap, tap of footsteps have turned into a consistent patter. Yelena keeps her in a death grip. Someone's making their way down the hall. They'll breach the room at any moment.

Destroy the package. That is what she's been told to do by the Cranes.

But she has a larger mission. The thought snakes through her mind, leaving fire in its wake. Her true mission is to figure out just what the American Outpost is up to.

The Cranes and Alexander Cady knew about this girl, but if they didn't tell Headquarters . . .

Surely Commander Starkovsky needs to know about this. And the best way to provide cold hard proof is in the form of the actual girl.

That would change her mission from *Destroy the package* to *Protect the package.*

Before Yelena can fully convince herself, the door bursts open.

"Get down, Yelena!" someone cries out, and *of course* it's Crystal, throwing code names to the wind. Yelena doesn't even have time to roll her eyes before she sees the flash of Crystal's glow bracelet as she flings a paring knife—where in the world did she get that, the kitchen?—toward the girl.

It's like Yelena's heart knows what she's going to do before she does. What a traitorous wretch of an organ. She grabs the girl and twists to protect her, which means the knife embeds itself into *Yelena's* side, right under her rib cage. The girl lets out a surprised squeak, her eyes fixing on the blood suddenly welling. She swallows convulsively.

Destroy the package. Protect the package.

"Oh my gosh!" Crystal cries out. "I didn't mean—" She staggers back as Yelena pulls the knife out of her hip with a wince, blood dripping from the sharp point, before taking a step toward her.

"That hurt," Yelena says.

"I didn't mean to! You got in the way!" Crystal jerks her head toward the girl. "Hello? Grab her! What are you doing?"

Yelena looks down at the knife. *Drip, drip, drip* goes the blood.

She pockets the bloody knife and steps toward Crystal, who lets out a little shudder and stumbles back.

Destroy the package.

Another step.

Protect the package.

One more step.

Time to decide, Belova.

She's right in front of her.

"*Yelena!* What are you doing?" Crystal demands.

"Honestly, Crystal," she says, "I have no idea."

She lashes out, grabbing Crystal's hand by her pointer and middle finger. Crystal barely has time to suck in a horrified breath—she doesn't have time to even form the word *no*—before Yelena snaps both fingers back with such sickening force that it elicits a scream that could crack glass. But she doesn't stop there: She's got ahold of Crystal's pinkie, and this time Crystal *does* get out a "No!" before Yelena breaks that finger, too, twisting her arm up and behind her, forcing her to the ground. Yelena darts forward, a Widow's Bite to the neck knocking Crystal out completely as her question echoes in Yelena's head.

What are you doing?

She pushes the door closed, flipping the lock, knowing it'll only take moments for one of her team members to blast it down.

She pulls off her sparkly belt, hooking it around the bedpost and pressing the little button under the buckle. Twenty stories is going to be cutting it close in terms of how long the rope hidden inside the belt will go, but it's better than nothing. Yelena jerks open the doors that lead to the balcony. Any second, her fellow trainees will breach the upstairs, drawn by Crystal's scream.

"Come," Yelena orders, looping the rope around her wrist and gesturing toward the girl.

"You're not safe! You don't have a pendant!" the girl starts, but Yelena slaps her hand into the girl's, yanking her closer.

"We can talk about jewelry later," Yelena says, jerking on the rope to make sure it's secure. "First, we need to survive."

Someone pounds on the door. "Yelena!" someone yells. Celia's voice.

Oh no. Not Celia. Yelena really doesn't want to hurt her. Which means she needs to get out of here.

"Time to go," Yelena says, even as the girl tries to scrabble free. "Hold on tight if you don't want to die."

She grabs the girl by the waist and lifts, running toward the balcony as the bedroom door breaks open. She leaps up onto the ledge, and the child screams as she sees how high up they are.

"Yelena!" Celia shouts as she catches sight of them.

Yelena looks back, her arm tight around the girl's waist.

"Sorry," she says to Celia. "Looks like you're about to lose another roommate."

And then she jumps off the high-rise.

8.
THIRD STREET

LOCATION: NEW YORK CITY
OBJECTIVE: PROTECT THE PACKAGE

The falling is as close to freedom as a girl like Yelena can get. The wind rushes through her hair, the world blurs, the child's scream fills her ears over the zip of the rope unfolding as they soar down, the ground getting closer and closer.

Shooting pains rip through Yelena's shoulder as they both jerk to a stop.

They've run out of rope, but, looking down, they're only about ten feet above the ground.

Think fast, Belova.

She lets go, holding the girl tightly. They both hit the ground at a roll and Yelena pushes the girl to her feet quickly.

The girl sways on the spot, like she's about to vomit. Yelena has no time for such nerves, so she leaps to her feet and grabs her.

"Run!" Yelena yells. Her teammates will already be on the move, heading to the lobby of the Stanley. They need to get off the street and hide.

As soon as that idea comes, Yelena's rejecting it. She won't let them trap her like a rat in a cage, and that's what this city is. If they don't move now, before one of her teammates calls in reinforcements, they'll never get out of New York.

Three blocks down from the Stanley, she finally starts to slow, partly because Crystal stabbed her a little and partly because the girl stumbles, clutching her side like she's got a stitch.

"You have to let me go back!" the girl pants. "They'll hurt my—"

"Your handler is fine. You're the one they want," Yelena interrupts, looking up and down the street, trying to find an easy target. She wants a vehicle with some heft; a tiny car isn't good in a situation where you have to mow someone down properly.

"Please, just let me go," the girl says.

"We need to get out of here," Yelena says, ignoring her pleas as she spots the perfect opportunity. Just down the street in front of an old brownstone house, an expensive-looking woman is getting out of a sleek minivan with a net bag of soccer balls tossed over her shoulder.

"I promise I won't tell anyone you got me out," the girl babbles.

"So helpful, when my entire team saw me take you,"

Yelena says. "Come *on*. Stop trying to impede the process of rescuing you."

She tugs the girl across the street, timing it perfectly so she runs into the woman heading toward the brownstone's steps. The bag of soccer balls knocks into Yelena's stomach and the woman loses hold of it. Yelena reaches out, grabbing the end of the bag before soccer balls go bouncing all over the sidewalk.

"Oh my, amazing reflexes!" the woman exclaims as she stops, not noticing in the bustling chaos as Yelena's hand slips into the pocket of her white linen blazer and lifts her car keys.

"I'm so sorry!" Yelena says. "I wasn't looking where I was going."

"It's all right," says the woman, taking the bag back from Yelena. "Thanks for the save."

She disappears into her brownstone. Yelena sighs in relief, her hand still tight around the girl's. Yelena drags the girl into the street, eyes on the driver's seat of the minivan, worried that if she lets go of her even for a second she'll run and cause even more problems.

A press of a button on the key fob unlocks the minivan.

"Wait! We're *stealing*?" the girl asks.

"Of course we are!"

Yelena's reaching toward the door with her free hand

when suddenly the girl's hand slips away. Yelena whirls, an annoyed remark on her lips quickly disappearing.

The girl's fallen to the ground, hit so hard with a tranquilizer dart that she is knocked back a few steps, a shallow cut on her forehead.

"Belova!" shouts a voice. It's not one of her teammates. At least not one of the ones she came with.

"Well, she healed fast," Yelena mutters to herself. Johanna clearly has a harder head than she thought. She turns to see her striding down the street, the tranquilizer gun pointed at Yelena's chest. But all Yelena can see is red, creeping along her vision.

"That's a full-size dart!" Yelena yells. "You could kill her!"

"That's the point, dummy!" Johanna yells back. "What in the world are you doing? Crystal started jabbering over the radio to the backup team that you'd lost your mind. That you must've encountered some sort of mind-control gas."

"You hurt the girl," Yelena says, unable to focus on anything else.

Johanna's eyes widen. "What are you—"

Yelena learned several weaknesses of Johanna's during their fight. One of which is that there is some old injury to her right shoulder. She dodged a little too fast away from blows coming from that side, like she was afraid someone would make contact.

So Yelena makes contact. She drives her fist straight into Johanna's shoulder. The girl pitches forward with a pained grunt, caught by surprise, and Yelena grabs a handful of her hair and smashes her head into the side of the minivan. Her forehead bounces off the metal and she falls back into the street, dazed and coughing as the air's knocked out of her.

Yelena picks up the little girl, placing her in the back seat, carefully buckling her up. Celia would be proud.

"Yelena!" A shrill scream grabs her attention before she can climb into the driver's seat. Celia's at the end of the block, Tiffany and Crystal trailing after her.

"If you do this, you're dead," Johanna sputters out.

Yelena shrugs. "We're all dead in the end."

She climbs into the minivan, pressing the ignition button as Celia and the rest of her teammates grow closer and closer in the rearview.

Yelena pulls into the street and floors it.

9.
ON THE ROAD

LOCATION: NEW YORK STATE
OBJECTIVE: INTERROGATE THE PACKAGE

For the first thirty minutes or so, she drives one-handed, using the paring knife Crystal had thrown at her to unhook the radio from her molar before digging the tracking chip out of her neck. She leaves the chip and radio somewhere in New York, and then she's driving for hours, no thinking, just *Drive, put miles between you and them*, and suddenly they're forty miles from the Ohio border, the blood on her neck long dried and the van nearly out of gas.

Now she has to plan.

Gas first. She passes a sign. There's a station in ten miles.

That unfortunately gives her ten miles to think. Which leads Yelena to the question:

What have I done?

The question circles in her head as the headlights of the minivan cut through the darkness. She presses hard on the gas, and she'd like to pretend she's not avoiding her dark thoughts, but she's a little too honest with herself. She has to be. Because . . .

What have I done?

Her eyes skitter to the rearview mirror, where she can see the girl passed out in the back seat where Yelena threw her, the mark from the tranquilizer dart a livid red on her neck.

She remembers waking up in the Red Room for the first time with a mark like that. She was younger than this girl looks.

What will the Red Room do to her now?

Yelena doesn't know which *her* she's thinking of. Herself? Or the girl? The little her-but-not-her.

They are not one and the same. She must remember that. This girl . . .

The package. The words slither into her mind in a voice that's not hers. Almost as soon as she thinks it, she rejects it. She's a *child*.

But is she? Are any of them?

She can barely tear her eyes away from her, now that there is no accusing and familiar blue staring back at her. She forces her gaze back onto the road, trying to ignore the question simmering under her skin.

What have I done?

Yelena pulls into the gas station and comes to a stop in front of one of the pumps. She has a hundred-dollar bill on her and nothing else. She checks the rearview again—the girl is still sleeping off the tranquilizer dart, her chest rising and falling steadily. Yelena tries to tamp down the burning curl of anger she feels again, thinking about that. Those darts were filled with enough tranquilizer to knock out a grown man. It was dangerous to hit a little girl with one.

But that was Johanna's aim, wasn't it? To be dangerous? To kill the package?

That was the mission. And Yelena has failed.

It's not the real mission, she reminds herself. The real mission is finding the truth about the girl with her face and revealing whatever they're up to at the American Outpost. Is the Outpost monitoring successful Widows' families? Recruiting from them for some reason? Are the American Widows so breakable that they have to seek out bloodlines from Headquarters instead?

But Yelena has seen Johanna fight. Seen how Celia sprang into action. How Tiffany kept calm when the plan changed so much—and kept everyone else calm. Even Crystal, as breakable as her name, landed a blow on Yelena.

She is starting to understand it isn't the Outpost's

trainees that are the problem, like the Commander worries.

It's the teachers.

That means whatever orders the Cranes have given her are not the right ones. The Commander trusts her judgment and skills. That's why he sent her here to collect intel.

And collecting information is exactly what she's doing. As soon as she has enough, she'll contact the Commander and explain everything.

It will be enough. She'll see to it.

It *has* to be enough. The alternative . . .

A shudder runs through Yelena. Her eyes burn like she's back in that room, strapped to the chair, unable to blink as images assault her. One after another until it turns into a violent blur. Until pain—hers or others'—means so much less because she's seen so much of it, as their words, their instructions, their subliminal messages drill into her so deep she's not sure she'll ever get them out.

She flinches. Where did that thought come from?

Of course she'll never get them out. She doesn't want them out. That's absurd. She accepted that truth and her role a long time ago. The goal can only be to walk in the cracks of the world, not on the carefully laid roads of it.

She belongs to the Red Room, not the world. She exists in the between space, in a reality only the real players of the universe know of. The Red Room put her there, gave her the privilege to see the layers of the world, the true workings of it. They gave her a place, a role, a purpose.

They took you, just like you took this girl.

She banishes that thought as well, getting out of the van and pushing the button on the door so that the sliding passenger door whisks open with a soft chime.

It's not enough to wake the girl. Yelena nudges her lightly and then more firmly, just to be sure she's completely out. Once she's assured herself, she carefully unhooks the pendant around the girl's neck. *You're not safe. You don't have a pendant.* That's what she had said in the penthouse.

Yelena lays the pendant on the flat of her palm, examining it. It almost looks like someone stamped an old wax seal into a puddle of silver instead of wax. The impression of an owl is on one side; on the other, an olive branch, a phrase stamped above it: THE ORDER OF MINERVA.

Yelena pockets the necklace and grabs her emergency cash. Heading into the little store attached to the gas station, Yelena makes sure to keep her hood up, but the woman at the register doesn't even look up when she comes in.

When push comes to shove, a person really can whittle themselves down to the basics: Vehicle. Fuel. Food. Water. Warmth.

If you have those things and you know how, you can move through the world very quietly. That's her aim, though her mind is the opposite of quiet as she stares at the rows of chips without really seeing them. Her brain keeps circling around *Sister?* and *Why would she be here, of all places?* and *What did the Outpost want with her?*

Had they taken the girl from her mother?

Their mother?

Yelena doesn't know why she's so sure it's *mother* instead of *father*. It's not like she can remember which parent she takes after.

It's not like she can remember if she even knew either of her parents. Not for sure. The Red Room told her she was given up. But the girls, they sometimes trade stories at night.

Yelena hadn't been very old when she put together that they told *all* of them that they had been given up. Some days she believed it. Other days, she told herself she was a naive fool to think the Red Room wouldn't just take what they wanted.

Is it better to think she was taken rather than abandoned? If she is honest with herself—and sometimes she is—she must admit she doesn't know. They both seem heartbreaking in different ways, and is that not what life is? A series of choices that lead down different paths of pain?

Isn't it better that the Red Room taught her a different way? One of power?

After all, her broken memories, the ones that show up in dreams, who knows what they really mean. Who knows who that woman she never reaches is. Maybe the memories were implanted by the Red Room to confuse her. To test her.

Is *this* a test?

Her hand freezes in the act of reaching out for a bag of something called Funyuns as the thought hits her. Is this one of Victor Crane's tests to get back at her for her "attitude," as he called it?

Her fingers close around the bag and she pulls it off the shelf. Well, if it is a test, she's certainly failed it.

She tosses the bag into the canvas tote bag she found in the van. It declares she's a proud parent of an honor student at Talbot Academy on the front. She grabs a few different kinds of chips, adding a bag of jerky before moving on to the candy section. By the time she's made her way through the soda case, she's got quite the stash. She hesitates in front of the row of tiny bottles of vodka. Cleaning her wound thoroughly is a priority. Infection can take down even the healthiest of people fast. Making sure the cashier is looking the other way, she slips a bottle into her pocket.

The instinct is strong to steal the rest of her haul, but she fights that, going up to the front and letting the cashier check her out.

"Can I also get fifty dollars of unleaded on pump three?" Yelena asks.

"Of course, have a great day!" the cashier chirps, and Yelena gives her a nod before grabbing the tote bag and heading back to the parking lot. She starts to fill the tank before tossing the bag across the console so it lands on the passenger seat.

Once the pumping is finished, she climbs back behind the wheel and reaches up to adjust the mirror.

She freezes.

The back seat is empty.

She's *gone*. How has Yelena lost her already?

"What the—"

Yelena dashes out of the van, looking around wildly, trying to spot her. She doesn't have very long legs; she can't have gotten too far.

"If an eight-year-old outsmarts me . . ." she mutters, hating that she has to guess a direction, no reason, no plan, no logic behind it.

There's a park on the other side of the street. She pelts across the road and onto the path leading into the greenery. There's a spot of white ahead, and as she runs faster, she sees it's a gazebo.

And what do you know, the girl is sitting in it like she's waiting for someone.

It's definitely not Yelena, because the second she sees her, she leaps to her feet and starts running again.

"Get away from me!"

Yelena dashes across the grass, catching up to her easily now that she's in her sights. She grabs the girl by the arm.

"Stop it!" the girl hisses. "Let go of me!"

"Hey," Yelena says. "I saved you from an assassination attempt! Do you even know what that is? You could at least say thank you. Plus I bought you snacks with my limited funds. This is how you repay me?"

"Get away! You don't have a pendant."

"You're quite obsessed with these pendants," Yelena says, reaching into her pocket and pulling out the one she took off her. She lets it dangle, swinging in the air between them. The girl sucks in a startled breath, her hand going to her throat, realizing hers is gone.

"Give that back to me!"

She snatches for it. Yelena raises it out of her reach. The girl growls. It's such a familiar sound that it has

Yelena staring again, tracing the girl's face with her gaze, wondering *how* they can be so similar. Sisters share traits, of course. But usually sisters are raised together.

She was not raised with this girl. And she is fully convinced she was not raised *like* this girl. Maybe the growling is similar, but Yelena would never cry. She would never have hesitated before stealing the van or taking the knife. Yelena would've taken the knife when offered and been grateful for it.

"Explain to me what the pendant means," Yelena says. "The woman in the hall. She had one, too. Who is Minerva?"

"If you don't know what it means, you don't get an explanation," the girl says, maddeningly. "Now give it back. And . . . and let me go. I . . . I thank you for helping me. But I have to go now. I have places to be."

"Have a busy work week, do you? What are you, seven?" Yelena asks.

"I'm eight," the girl snarls, like any eight-year-old who has been accused of being merely seven.

"A mountain of a difference, those twelve months," Yelena says. "And how far do you think you're going to get, Little Miss Eight-Year-Old, with no money and no shoes, I might add?" She looks down at the girl's feet. "At least let's find you some shoes."

"No!" the girl says, even though Yelena thinks she's

being entirely reasonable. "Stay away from me! Don't try to pretend. I know you! I know what you are."

There's a spark of fear in the girl's eyes that Yelena didn't recognize until this moment. It's been there since she approached her in the park, but she didn't realize.

She misread the situation.

Yelena goes very still, making sure she doesn't make any sudden movements. Her Widow's Bite bracelet is still on her wrist. If she has to, she can knock the girl out.

But wouldn't that be proving her accusation? That Yelena is a Widow?

"Who do you think I am?" Yelena asks calmly, keeping her gaze steady, her body language loose instead of alert. *Don't scare her off.*

The girl lets out a shaky laugh that's laced with pure terror. It makes Yelena's skin prickle, like someone's rolling a wheel of rusty nails across it. Yelena saved her. . . . Why is the girl so scared of her?

"*You* know who you are," the girl says. "*I* know who you are! They told us about you. They warned us. You're *the Source.*"

The way she says it, so hushed and heavy with importance, it's supposed to hang there between them, break apart some facade. The girl sucks in a breath, shaky and waiting for some ax to fall on her.

Instead, Yelena frowns.

She tilts her head in genuine confusion, and she sees that confusion mirrored in the girl's face.

"What's the Source?" Yelena asks.

10.
THE BUNKER

LOCATION: SOMEWHERE IN THE DESERT

The Doctor has always loved the sound of her heels clicking down the cavernous halls of Home Base. There's something about the echo, how it bounces off the cement walls of the underground facility like it can't quite escape.

Just like her subjects.

There is something about trapped things. When she was a girl, she kept moths in mason jars to study them, then moved on to mice. Her mother scolded her for the mice like there was a difference. She had poked holes in the tops, after all, just like with the moths. But it upset Mother. *They need more room, darling*, Mother told her.

But did they really? Not if you shape the subject's world from the start. If they never know freedom, they never crave it. That had been her hypothesis.

The Heart Subject has proved it wrong. That girl . . .

She was a mistake from the start. The Triple H

project—Hand, Heart, and Head—started out as the *Double* H project—just Hand and Head were her focus. Strength and Mind are where her interests have lain. The Doctor let herself be convinced to add a third branch to an experiment that was originally restricted to the body and the mind. A subject focused on each. When Director Cady suggested adding a third, a subject focused on emotions—or the heart—she of course went along with it. The man controlled her funding, after all. But eight years later, she is filled with nothing but regret. The Heart Subject has nearly destroyed an already tenuous balance between the subjects. All because her emotions were catered to instead of controlled, like the other two subjects'.

Love is an infection. And the Doctor knows what to do with infection. You cut it out, by any means necessary.

It matters not, now, the Doctor reminds herself. Director Cady saw reason and gave the order himself. It's been taken care of. She can finally continue her work without the Heart Subject getting into the others' ears with her nonsense.

The Doctor swishes down to the end of corridor B, her blue tweed pencil skirt an exact shade match to the cashmere cardigan with the mother-of-pearl buttons she's tied over her shoulders. She reaches the end of the hall, examining herself in the picture window–size mirror set into the wall. Not a hair out of place from her simple French twist, her gold stud earrings tasteful. She wore hoops, once upon a time. The Hand Subject ripped one from her lobe last year.

The Doctor noted the unusual strength the Hand Subject had exhibited as blood poured down her neck. She made sure to fix the moment that had triggered such a violent reaction in her mind in case she needed such a response again. Before she allowed the medics to clean her up, she carefully recorded everything in her ever-present notebook as the men in white subdued the screaming subject.

She was careful not to wear hoop earrings again. The Doctor is nothing if not circumspect after being taught a lesson. She wishes her subjects were the same, but alas, they have lessons still to learn.

The Doctor presses a button at the edge of the mirror. A slight shimmer, and then her reflection disappears, exposing the two-way mirror and the room behind it.

There are toys strewn across the padded floor. She's never approved of the toys, but she's settled on them as a lesser evil. They wanted books beyond the schoolbooks that she's created for them. That will not do, not after what happened the first time she allowed such liberties with literature. They got ideas.

Her little mice must be kept snug in their mason jars. They are not for this world. They serve a much greater purpose.

Her eyes settle on her two remaining subjects. They're tucked in a corner, blond heads bent together, tapping, always tapping to each other. Their silent little language. A code she has not been able to break. Sometimes the Doctor is desperate to know what they're saying. Sometimes, they switch to some sort of made-up language just to annoy her. Twin-speak of a sort. She's heard of such linguistic phenomena.

She'll find a way to break their code someday. They can't hide from her forever.

Her job is to know everything about them. To form them into everything the experiment demands.

Her little mice will be even stronger now that she's cut the weak link from the far superior specimens.

The Doctor presses her hand against the glass.

The Hand Subject's head snaps toward the mirror in their playroom. The Doctor's arm tenses, but she refuses to snatch her hand away.

The Doctor's right ear aches from the memory of the girl ripping out her earring.

The Hand Subject rises to her feet. Shoulders squared, already so intimidating, so sure of herself at eight years old.

The Doctor watches as her subject charges forward with a hellish scream. She slams her fists against the glass, pounding beats punctuated by one demand:

"Give her back! Give her back! Give her back!"

11.
THE PARK

LOCATION: PENNSYLVANIA
OBJECTIVE: DISCOVER WHAT THE SOURCE IS

"**W**hat's the Source?" Yelena asks again.

The girl with her face stares at Yelena like she thinks it's a trick.

"Seriously, I have no idea what you're talking about," Yelena says. "Do you even know my name?"

The girl shakes her head. "I don't need to know your name. I've seen your picture. That's enough. You're the Source."

"I still don't know what that means," Yelena says. "Are you going to try to run away again?"

The girl looks over her shoulder like she's trying to estimate whether or not it's worth it. It's strange, to see thoughts play across a younger, more open version of her face. This girl has not been taught to control her emotions the way Yelena has.

"I have places to be," the girl tries again.

"You have things to explain," Yelena says. "Like this Source business. It's not every day a girl like me discovers she has some sort of code name she didn't know about. I'm dying of curiosity. Why don't you explain it all to me over a breakfast of onion-flavored snacks and fruit punch?"

The girl's mouth screws up in distaste. "That sounds like a terrible combination."

"Well, walk back to the van and see the snacks I bought, and you can come up with a better combination," Yelena says. "Or you can try to top my gross combination if you wish. I did purchase the only kind of hot sauce the store had."

"Hot sauce?"

"A friend recently introduced me to it," Yelena says, ignoring the pang she feels thinking about Celia's betrayed expression right before Yelena leapt off the balcony. "Don't they have it where you're from? My friend made it sound like everywhere in America has it."

"I don't think so. Or maybe they just didn't give it to us."

Yelena carefully doesn't jump on this bit of information the girl offers.

They. Us.

The girl is wary enough of Yelena, what with this Source fear of hers. Yelena will get more information with the carrot over the stick. Especially with a girl who cries as much as this one.

"We could try putting it on some things," Yelena says.

"It makes your mouth burn in the best way. But you have to come back to the van."

"I have places to be," the girl says a third time, but it's accompanied by a stomach rumble that could put a grizzly bear to shame.

Yelena raises her eyebrow pointedly. "Give me a half hour to feed you," she says. "And find you some shoes. I think there might be some in the back of the van. Then we can find a phone and you can call someone to take you to your places to be, okay?"

The girl hesitates. "I know how to fight," she says suddenly. "I will bite you if I have to."

"That sounds terrifying," Yelena says.

Her brow wrinkles like she thinks Yelena is joking.

"Mouths are dirty," Yelena explains. "Biting is an excellent long-term way to infect the enemy. Sometimes infection even kills. Keep it in your arsenal. But maybe don't use it against me. Since I'm not the enemy here, what with the whole saving-your-life thing I did earlier. Come on, then."

She turns and starts walking out of the park, hoping the girl will follow. *Carrot*, she reminds herself. *Not the stick.*

The stick is just so much *easier* most of the time.

But her instincts pay off. She gets nearly halfway down the path before the girl moves. She trots after

Yelena, the lure of snacks too great to resist. They have that in common, at least. Yelena is careful not to speak or push the rest of the walk back, just in case she scares the funny little bird.

When they get back to the van, Yelena spreads the snack haul along the back seat, sitting back and watching the girl pick through the food with interest.

Some of the packages and brands seem more obscure to the girl than even Yelena, which is another interesting bit of information to collect. From the way she speaks, she's clearly American. Her vowels flatten instead of round like Yelena's do when speaking English. She, of course, can do an American accent when needed. She has always been praised for her ear for dialects. But the girl isn't doing an accent. She's speaking like a little American because that's what she is. Or at least, that's who raised her.

Maybe they just didn't give it to us.

That's what she said when Yelena mentioned hot sauce. Who are *they*?

And just as importantly: What did she mean by *us*?

"These are good," Yelena says, pushing the cheese puffs toward the girl. "What's your name?"

The girl slants her a look before taking the cheese puffs. She waits until Yelena pops a puff into her mouth before she does the same.

So she's been taught about poison, then. And taught to be wary of it. Interesting.

"You said this mysterious *they* of yours . . . they didn't tell you my name? Aren't you curious? We could trade. Mine for yours."

"You would do that?"

"I would," Yelena says. "Do you want me to go first?"

Build trust, she tells herself. That is key when bringing in an asset. Especially one who has a preexisting idea of you. *The Source* is a specific kind of code name. A dehumanizing one. Designed to separate her from it, strip her of anything but whatever myth they told this girl.

If this girl doesn't see her as a person, there's no way Yelena can make her think of her as a person she can trust.

Offer something to get something. It's a simple little trick.

The girl nods.

"I'm Yelena," Yelena says.

The girl pops another cheese puff into her mouth, chewing thoughtfully as she considers her.

"I'm Subject H3," the girl says finally. There's a smug gleam in her eyes, one that tells Yelena she planned this all along.

Yelena lets out a huff of laughter, because if she doesn't laugh, she might give into slapping the girl's arm. Gently. Well . . . Widows don't exactly *do* gentle. But more gently than she normally would slap someone.

Actually, she can't remember the last time she did something as silly as dole out a slap.

She moved on to much more lethal means long ago, and it never bothered her until this moment as she stares at her hands, resisting an urge that maybe shouldn't be directed at this girl—at Subject H3—at all.

There are many people in this world who deserve Yelena Belova's violence. But she is almost certain this girl is not one of them.

Subject H3. The girl has told her all sorts of things without meaning to, using such wording. Her mind turns over it as the girl grabs another cheese puff, swiping the bottle of hot sauce from its place between them on the back seat, dribbling a generous amount on the snack before popping it in her mouth. Her eyes water at the bite of the spice, but she doesn't seem to regret it, because she's already reaching for another puff, bottle in hand and at the ready.

"Surely you have a real name," Yelena says casually. "You're a girl, not a science experiment."

The girl stiffens next to her, too young and unpracticed to hide it.

"What does your mother call you?" Yelena asks.

"We don't have one of those," she says.

We again. She said *they told us* about the Source. She keeps slipping into the plural, almost unknowingly. It sends an increasing tension snaking through Yelena's gut. She wants to ask *Who is we?* But she dances away from the question like she's finally been given a map right in the middle of a minefield.

"No father, either?" Yelena guesses.

The girl shrugs, trying a hot sauce/gummy bear combo that has her eyes lighting up like a bonfire on the coldest, most pristine night of the year.

"Who takes care of you? You said you have seen my picture. Who showed it to you?"

She's quiet, like she's trying to pick the right words. "People at Home Base."

"What's Home Base?"

"It's . . . it's home," the girl says, and for once, it doesn't sound like she's being evasive on purpose.

"The woman in the penthouse . . . the one with the pendant. Was she one of the people who took care of you?"

At the mention of the woman, the girl tenses again. "Did you kill her?"

This time, Yelena doesn't give in too easily, even though the girl's voice cracks horribly. "Is she someone important to you?"

"Answer me," the girl orders, finally putting down the hot sauce bottle.

"Answer me, and I'll answer you," Yelena counters.

The girl glares. "You're the Source. Of course you killed her." She says it like she's convincing herself, even as her eyes beg Yelena to contradict her.

"You must have meant a lot to her," Yelena says. "For her to take you from your home and hire all that security to keep you safe."

"Please tell me it was quick," the girl blurts out. "Did you— Please tell me you didn't hurt her too—"

"She was not my mission," Yelena interrupts, because the girl's face is red—not from the spice—and she looks like she's about to pass out or breathe herself right into a panic attack.

"She's alive?"

"She'll have a big headache when she wakes up from the paralytic. But it was not my mission to kill her."

Yelena waits, but the girl just remains silent, like she's scared any words she speaks will lead to Yelena pulling more information out of her.

"Ask me what my mission was," Yelena prompts.

The girl takes her time, trying to see what the trap is. But Yelena is patient. She has age on her side, after all.

"What was your mission?" the girl asks grudgingly when she can find no trap.

That's the thing about truth. It's the kind of trap you can't see.

"My mission was to kill you," Yelena says, watching the girl's face carefully. There was a little bit of cheese-puff orange at the corner of her mouth. "But I didn't do that, did I?"

"You— Maybe you just saved me to kill me. Maybe you're lying in wait," the girl says.

That gets another laugh out of Yelena. "That would make me terrible at my job."

"Maybe you are," the girl says, edging toward the door like she doesn't know what child locks are. Yelena sends up a prayer of thanks for paranoid soccer moms.

Yelena shakes her head. "I'm not."

"Then why didn't you kill me?"

"You look like me," Yelena says, because it's the truth, but it's also not. "Do you see it?"

A wary, weighted silence, and then: a shaky nod.

They sent you. Why would they send you?

The woman's confused words in the penthouse echo in Yelena's ears as her mind hovers on the edge of some sort of realization she still can't grasp.

She doesn't *want* to grasp it. Because if this girl is not a sister or a niece or a cousin or some sort of relative . . .

She has Yelena's face. Her *exact* face. She gave Yelena a subject number instead of a name. And if Yelena is *the Source* . . .

The question becomes: The Source of *what*?

"What did they tell you about me?" Yelena asks. "The people at Home Base."

"That you were dangerous."

"Well, they are right," Yelena says, and the girl's mouth drops open like she wasn't expecting such an easy admission. The girl wears *everything* on her face. Yelena wonders if she was ever like that. Did the Red Room train it out of her? Or was it never there in the first place if you arrive at the Red Room with a carefully wiped blank slate?

"You saw proof of how dangerous I am last night yourself. I am a great threat. To my enemies."

The girl's eyes fill with tears. "You're the Source. Which means *I'm* your enemy," she whispers, like it's the most awful thing in the world, and Yelena can't help but wonder, if she actually believes it, *why* oh *why* would she say it?

This girl is such a funny little thing. Too trusting and too wary in the wrong ways, not knowing which way is up.

"Well, if we're enemies, I at least deserve to know the name of my enemy, don't I?" Yelena asks.

The girl rolls her eyes. "You're the worst," she says. And then she offers it up like a crumb of bread to a greedy duck: "I'm Leni."

Leni. Yelena swallows with a click around the name like it's the last bit of confirmation she needs.

Subject H3. Does that mean there are three of them? That Leni is just third in a series of . . . how many?

Oh god, how many are there? She forces herself away from panic, from the thought of *dozens* or some equally terrible number. Three is already . . .

Three is way too many.

"You're not my enemy, Leni," Yelena says.

Subject H3. Home Base. Why would they send you?

How has this become her life? If she hadn't knocked Johanna out, she'd still be at the Outpost, oblivious.

Is it better not to know? Yelena can't answer. Because she knows.

"I think you know exactly what you are, don't you?" Yelena asks.

Leni sniffs again, nodding as her eyes shimmer with tears that Yelena is sure she never shed at that age.

"I'm one of your clones."

12.
THE PARKING LOT

LOCATION: PENNSYLVANIA
OBJECTIVE: DO NOT FREAK OUT

*Y*ou *must stay calm.*

Yelena doesn't want to. It takes every shred of training—and the memory of the punishment that followed every error—to keep herself from tumbling right out of the minivan and throwing up cheese puffs all over the parking lot.

Yelena forces herself to breathe—and stem the flow of the hundreds of questions she currently has. Overwhelming Leni won't help. She might try to run again, and then Yelena won't have any information at all . . . like who did this. And *why*.

"Are you going to kill me now?"

She grits her teeth against how *resigned* her clone sounds to death. Almost like she won't even put up a good fight. Is she *sure* this girl has her genetics?

"If I were going to kill you, I would've done it in the penthouse," Yelena says. "I do not go to the bother of rappelling off high-rises with someone I rescued only to kill them after all that trouble. That's a waste of time.

Killing should be efficient—make a note of that. Plus, I turned on my team for you. Why would I kill you?"

"You did break a lot of that girl's fingers," Leni says thoughtfully, as if this is the deciding factor of loyalty.

"She deserved that," Yelena says. "She stabbed me."

"Only a little. And accidentally, it looked like."

"Are you actually defending Crystal?" Yelena asks, astonished. "She encouraged me to kill you! If she had found you first, she would've tried to murder you. I'm a little skeptical that she would've succeeded against even an eight-year-old version of myself, but who knows, maybe she would've landed a lucky blow."

"She got you, and you're *way* older than me," Leni mutters.

"Barely! And I got her back!"

"You didn't *stab* her back, though, you just made her scream a lot."

"She has very breakable bones! I was using the intel I gathered to my advantage like any good spy. You should take a page out of my book, tiny me."

"I am not you." Leni scowls.

"The science of the cloning process says otherwise. We are genetically identical."

"I'm not like you," Leni says. "You have no idea what you're talking about."

"Then why don't you explain it to me?" Yelena asks.

"We're . . . we're *better* than you," Leni says finally. "That's the whole point."

"Of the experiment?" Yelena asks, because it has to be one, if Leni's a test subject.

"It's not— The Doctor doesn't like it when we call it that," Leni says.

Yelena schools her face into a placid, mostly disinterested mask. "Is this doctor of yours in charge?"

Leni nods.

"And how many . . ." Yelena pauses, trying to think about how to phrase it. "You keep saying *we*," she says finally.

That spark of fear is back in the girl's eyes, like it never left, like it was just waiting to flare back to life, as she realizes what she's given away.

She is *so* different from Yelena. It's strange to watch the emotions flit across her face instead of being locked up in neat boxes in her mind. . . .

It's like watching a life Yelena never had a chance at. What in the world has this experiment wrought on this version of herself who cries and doesn't hide things and flinches like she doesn't know how to slide her mind away from her body and therefore the pain it feels?

"My sisters are none of your business," Leni says finally.

Sisters. Plural. That could mean any number. Yelena tries to quell the panic rising in her.

"Your sisters . . . do they cry as much as you?"

Leni glares at her. "My sisters would wipe the floor with you! Ellie made the Doctor bleed last year."

"How'd she do that?"

"She ripped her earring out," Leni says. "There was blood all over. She screamed and everything."

That sounds much more like her clone than this one.

"So, Ellie thinks on her feet," Yelena says. "And you're the soft one who cries and doesn't want to steal things."

Leni's eyebrows twitch in annoyance. "Stealing is wrong."

"It got us away from the people trying to kill us, didn't it?" Yelena asks.

"*You* are one of the people trying to kill me," Leni says.

"I was, until I changed my mind."

"That makes you the disloyal one, I think," Leni says, and Yelena's mouth snaps shut, her stomach clenching at being called out so directly.

"Are you loyal, Leni?" Yelena asks.

"I'm you, aren't I?" she asks mockingly. "So there's your answer."

"How many sisters do you have?"

The girl's cheeks burn. She says nothing.

"I think you're very loyal," Yelena says. "You're trying to protect them. That is the way of sisters, is it not? That's what I've been told, at least."

"You don't have any sisters," Leni says, almost as if in realization.

"Even if I did, I would not know it," Yelena says. "Just like I wouldn't know my mother's face, even if we were in the same room together."

There's pity in the girl's eyes. Yelena doesn't like it one bit. "That's one of the reasons the Doctor was there when we were born. She said that she wanted to shape us from the start. They had to take your memories before they could shape you."

"They made me what I needed to be, to become who I am," Yelena says.

"A blank slate has to be wiped fully clean," Leni says. "Are you sure it is? Because that is the Doctor's theory, you know. That none of you are fully clean slates. That the memories, the instincts, they linger. The right trigger . . ." She snaps her fingers, and Yelena *hates* herself, because she flinches. And she knows her little mini me notices.

"The Doctor said that we'd be better if we were born in it, instead of brought into it," Leni tells her.

Yelena shifts, unsettled, trying not to think of her dreams. Of Celia's whispered confession that she has them, too.

"Why don't you hate them?" Leni asks. "They took away what made you *you*."

Yelena can't ask herself such a dangerous question. Can't even let it dwell on her lips or in her mind for more than a split second before she boxes it away, locking it up in the deepest parts of herself before there can be even a glimmer of an answer.

"Do you hate this Doctor of yours?" Yelena says. "Do you hate your home? Or did you leave it and your sisters willingly . . . happily?"

"I don't hate the Doctor," Leni says. "I don't think I hate anyone. But I'm pretty sure the Doctor hates me."

Yelena frowns, but she doesn't push, waiting for more words to spill out between them.

"She said it wasn't working," Leni confesses. "That I was messing everything up. I was the weak link."

"In the experiment? Leni, what exactly are they . . ." Yelena looks her up and down, suddenly assessing. She's skinny, but not in a malnourished way. There are no signs of scars from what Yelena can see, but that doesn't really mean anything.

There are many ways to hurt someone and never leave a mark.

"What were they doing to you?" Yelena asks.

Leni lets out a big sigh, and Yelena can tell she's slowly giving in.

"Heart. Head. Hand," Leni says. "The Doctor raised us each with a different focus. Ellie's the Hand. Her focus is physical. She's . . . she's so strong. And faster than anyone. She barely feels pain."

"She's the one who ripped the Doctor's earring out," Yelena says.

"Yes, but the Doctor deserved it," Leni says, like a confession. It sends a little thrill of triumph through Yelena, immediately followed by a sour feeling she refuses to call shame.

The girl is starting to trust her. That's what she wants.

"Leah's the Head," Leni continues.

"Let me guess: Leah's the smart one," Yelena says.

Leni nods. "She can solve any problem. She reads all the books the Doctor makes for us. Even the Doctor says her mind is brilliantly strategic."

"I'm guessing the Doctor isn't big on praise?" Yelena asks.

"She thinks compliments make you lazy," Leni says.

"So, your sisters . . . there are two of them?" Yelena asks, and when Leni nods, Yelena feels both relieved that it's just three of them and also like screaming because *three clones* is three too many clones. There should be no clones. Did she do this by being the best? Did the American Outpost steal her DNA from Headquarters because their Widows are so lacking they decided they need to grow some from home?

It seems like such an effort when one could just kill the Crane brothers and actually hire some competent trainers. But the Americans do have a curious and meandering way of going about some things.

"So that makes you the Heart," Yelena says. "So your focus is . . ."

"The emotional," Leni says. "Ellie and Leah . . . they were taught to bottle things up unless it helped their focus. But I—"

"You were told to feel everything."

Yelena suddenly understands the crying. She blinks rapidly, trying to hook her mind around it, because it seems . . .

Well, useless. Why would you steep a preteen girl in her *feelings* when you could focus her malleable mind on spycraft or languages or dozens of other useful things that aren't *emotions*?

"You look just like the Doctor," Leni says. "Like you think I'm useless."

Yelena looks down, her cheeks reddening, and hates her lack of control. Hates that even if she had it, this girl might see through it.

Because that's the thing about emotions and feelings. If you cut yourself off from them, they're a little harder to identify in others. You have to put effort into reading people. Into putting yourself in their shoes. It requires brainpower. It's not instinctual when you've hardened your own heart, no matter the training.

Leni's heart isn't hard. And she sees everything because she lets herself feel everything.

That kind of perception, it's almost prophetic.

It's not useless at all. It's dangerous if you're someone hiding things.

"She wanted to get rid of you, your Doctor," Yelena says. "Why didn't she just kill you?"

"Miss Bess," Leni says. "The woman at the hotel. She and Miss Irene took care of us at Home Base alongside the Doctor. When she heard that the Doctor was going to close the Heart part of the experiment, she gave me some sort of sleep medicine. I went to sleep at home and when I woke up, Miss Bess said we were at the Stanley Hotel and that I couldn't ever go back. That they'd kill me if I did."

"What was the plan after leaving the Stanley?"

Leni shakes her head. "I don't know," she says.

Yelena's skeptical gaze falls on her.

"I really don't! I promise," Leni repeats helplessly.

"I don't know yet if promises matter at all to you," Yelena says simply. She pulls out the pendant again, examining it. "Do you know what this is? What it means?"

Leni shakes her head. "All Miss Bess said was that the only people I could trust were people who had the pendant."

"Well," Yelena says, "I guess we'll have to figure out what it means, then."

"We will?"

"Yes, this is what we call *a clue*, little me."

"I told you, I'm not—"

"Are you going to sit back and learn some things, or are you going to argue with me?" Yelena asks. "If you've spent your entire life focused on emotions, that means . . . what . . . that you don't know how to research? How to throw a punch? How to do anything *but* feel?"

"I'm not useless," Leni snaps. "I can hit things. Just . . . not as well as Ellie. And I'm smart . . . just not as smart as Leah."

The defeated way she says it makes Yelena's stomach hurt. She tries to ignore it in favor of getting the snacks packed up. "You know, I think your Doctor is very shortsighted."

"Yeah?"

"Making you three focus on just one thing each like

your brains can't handle anything else? I mean, aren't I proof that we can multitask?"

Leni giggles. "She'd get really mad if you said that to her face."

"She seems like great company, your Doctor," Yelena says sarcastically. "She gives you a focus and makes your life about it and then tries to kill you for doing the very thing she assigned you to focus on? Talk about fickle. I thought scientists were supposed to be methodical."

"She said I gave my sisters bad ideas."

Yelena snorts. "I bet you did." She shoves the remaining bags of cheese puffs in one of the seemingly endless tote bags she unearthed in the back of the minivan. She has never thought about soccer moms being a prime car-stealing target, but the sheer amount of supplies they travel with is incredibly useful. She could probably live out of this van for a good week if she has to, now that she has acquired food. There's even a case of water bottles in the back.

As she moves to crawl back into the driver's seat, the wound on her hip stings in an ugly reminder that she intended to sew it up after she acquired food but got distracted by Leni running off. She glances down at her dark leggings. They hide the blood, but she needs to take care of it now. And the cut on Leni's cheek could use some stitching, too.

"Okay, first lesson," Yelena says, grabbing the dental floss and vodka she got in the mini-mart and the soccer mom's first-aid kit. "Always disinfect your wounds. Let's go clean up. If we walk around looking like we've been through a fight, we draw attention. We want to move through the world like ghosts. People see right through us."

Leni follows her across the parking lot and into the bathroom. Washing her hands, Yelena assesses the situation. Leni first. She uses the soccer mom's bleach wipes to clean the counter around the sink before lifting Leni to sit on it, the girl's legs dangling. She watches Yelena thoughtfully as she uncaps the vodka and douses a wad of paper towels with it. "This'll sting," Yelena warns.

Leni grits her teeth as Yelena presses the vodka-soaked towel to her forehead, cleaning the wound thoroughly. It's a bigger gash than she thought, now that the skin is clean of dried blood.

Johanna's going to pay for this. How dare she.

She was just doing her job . . . because you didn't. Yelena banishes the nasty voice, concentrating on cleaning the cut.

"You're being very tough," Yelena says. "We will have to sew it shut, though. Which brings us to the second lesson." She pulls out her own emergency kit, lifting the compact to reveal several mini tools tucked under the pan of "makeup," including the sewing needle that she selects. "Dental floss makes excellent thread to sew shut wounds. But a word of warning: Don't get the mint kind. It'll burn."

"Because of the menthol," Leni says immediately.

Yelena raises an eyebrow. "You sure you're not the smart one?" she asks, and the smile that Leni shoots her . . .

It's so proud it makes her stomach twist in a horribly guilty way.

The Doctor thinks compliments make you lazy.

The Doctor is an idiot. Even the Commander praises his Widows-in-training when they do something that exceeds his high expectations of them. It's what kept Yelena going some days. His praise was like a warm balm to a battered Widow's soul. The surge of anger she feels at the thought of these little girls locked up somewhere, starved of praise and forced to focus on one silly thing over everything else . . .

What a terrible way to raise fighters. To raise survivors. Because that's what a Widow is. A survivor.

Anyone who can survive the Red Room can survive anything. She tells herself that in the dead of night, when the dreams wake her, the ones that are worse than any nightmare or violent memory from a mission. The ones that promise a life—a lie—she can't remember.

"That's right, the menthol," Yelena says, because

Leni is looking at her expectantly, waiting for an answer. "So avoid the mint floss. And cinnamon. Just use plain."

"What if you don't have a needle?" Leni asks. She doesn't jerk as Yelena threads the needle into her skin. Yelena half expected her oh-so-sensitive clone to flinch away, but instead she holds herself very still, and Yelena finds that it's her own hands that are shaking.

"Superglue if you don't have a needle," Yelena says softly, trying to steady her own hands so she doesn't hurt the girl.

"Really?"

Yelena nods. "You can also heat up something metal—you have to get it red-hot—and cauterize the wound if it's bleeding too much. But I wouldn't do something like that with a scrape like this."

"It doesn't feel like a scrape."

"You're being very brave," Yelena says, tugging the edges of the cut closed and knotting the floss at the end. She washes her hands briskly and gently takes Leni's chin, turning her head to examine her handiwork. "Does it hurt?"

"I've had much worse," Leni echoes, and Yelena has to drop her hand from the girl's chin because her hands curl into fists, her nails biting into her palms as she fights for some calm in her mind.

"Do they hurt you?" she asks, the intensity she feels bleeding into the question.

"That's what they do," Leni says.

"You shouldn't— They shouldn't—" Yelena struggles, because what is she trying to say? She focuses on cleaning her own wound with the rest of the vodka and stitching the gash up with still-shaking hands. She'll have a scar to remind her of this. She doesn't know if she likes that idea.

"Do you do this a lot?" Leni asks.

"You'll have to be clearer about what 'this' is," Yelena says.

"Get hurt. Have to patch yourself up in dirty bathrooms on the run."

"Few times in a bathroom. Once in a ditch. A memorable time in an abandoned potato factory." Yelena wrinkles her nose. "Rotten potatoes smell terrible."

Leni cracks a smile reluctantly as Yelena grabs a small packet of antibiotic ointment from the first-aid kit, spreads it over the stitched cut, and adds a bandage to keep it clean. They've got Captain America's shield stamped on them in all its red, white, and blue glory. Yelena rolls her eyes at the sight. That guy is the definition of what Celia called a Goody Two-shoes.

"What are we gonna do next?" Leni asks as Yelena

sweeps the supplies back into the first-aid kit and zips it up.

"Next lesson of the day, little Leni: the power of the library."

Leni frowns; her head tilts. "What's a library?"

13.
THE LIBRARY

LOCATION: PENNSYLVANIA
OBJECTIVE: GATHER INTEL ON MINERVA

The look on Leni's face when they walk into the library is like that of someone seeing the ocean for the first time. Her eyes are so big they look like they're going to bug out of her face as they roam around the shelves of books.

"There's so many," she breathes. "I didn't realize there were so many books!"

"Oh, there are many more than this," Yelena says. "There's *billions* of books. You can even have thousands of them on a tablet and read them whenever you want."

"I didn't know," Leni says, and there's that uncomfortable pang in Yelena's chest again. She needs to push it down for good.

"Didn't you have books?" Yelena asks.

"Only ones that the Doctor wrote," Leni says. "Sometimes Miss Bess snuck us books from the outside. Some of them had pictures and everything. When the Doctor found out, she took them away. She said they gave us ideas. After that, we were only allowed the Doctor's books."

The Red Room's library is filled with books that Yelena had access to as a trainee. They were encouraged to fill their minds with the contents. But they were all books on spycraft and strategy and war. The politics of the day that she needs to know. Even the fiction they were given was so that they could converse in cultured situations . . . so that they could be better spies.

She never thought deeply on it, how carefully curated the library was. The books that *weren't* there.

What she was kept from.

But suddenly, it's all she can think of, watching Leni stare at the shelves of books like they hold the answers to the universe . . . because they do. They hold answers to a world she's never lived in, stuck in some desert bunker with that crazed Doctor of hers.

Yelena has to yank her fingernails out of her palms, the blood smearing on her leggings as she wipes her hands on them.

"Go ahead and look," she says, pushing Leni toward the children's section and then goes over to a computer that affords her a direct line of sight to Leni. She's not going to let her run away again.

Leni doesn't need to be told twice. She dashes over to

the shelves of books, standing in front of them like the sheer amount is overwhelming.

Yelena focuses on the computer screen, logging in to the web browser and pulling out the pendant to examine it once again.

She types `the Order of Minerva` into the search engine, but only a few hits show up about the Roman goddess. *Minerva is the goddess of wisdom*, Yelena reads, *and her symbols include an owl.*

She glances down at the pendant, tapping it against the desk. Then she types `"secret society" + "goddess minerva"` into the search bar.

More than a dozen sites pop up, including a social media post from a history account.

Posted by
@MYTHIC_HISTORY

Ever hear the rumor about Ada Lovelace being in a secret society of scientists? Let me tell you all about the Mothers of Minerva!

That's close to *Order of Minerva*. And Yelena knows better than anyone: History is written by the victors. Maybe the real name got obscured through the years.

Ada Lovelace lived in the 1800s, after all. Even Yelena knows about her. She's considered the first computer programmer.

Yelena scans through the history thread for intel, but it's not very helpful. The Mothers of Minerva, as this historian keeps calling it, doesn't really sound like a secret society in the usual sense—shadowy organizations that actually control the world—but more like a bunch of women in the 1800s who were probably a lot smarter than all the men around them and got sick of it, so they banded together in intellectual and scientific camaraderie.

"As they should," Yelena mutters. She scrolls to the bottom of the thread, where the historian states: *The Mothers of Minerva were disbanded in the 1920s.*

"Were they, though?" Yelena asks. She returns to the search engine. This time she has Ada Lovelace's name, so she pairs *Ada* with *"the order of minerva"* and *pendant* before clicking *search*.

Nothing comes up. She's about to click out when she notices that there *is* something in the image search tab. With a frown, she toggles over to the image. It's a picture of a woman with an owl on her shoulder and purple-red flowers sprouting at her feet. Yelena clicks on the source of the image, which brings her to a website that is just an ISP number and looks like it was made in the ancient early days of the internet. The image is centered on the web page, *Minerva, Goddess of Wisdom* typed in a lurid green—in Comic Sans, of all fonts—above it.

Yelena scrolls down. There's nothing else on the site but the image of the goddess with her owl companion, flowers at her feet. She hovers the cursor over it and clicks, but nothing happens. Yelena's about to click away when she sees it: the pendant hanging around Minerva's neck.

She clicks directly on the pendant and is suddenly prompted for a password. Yelena's mind races through the possibilities. Something to do with the goddess? Something to do with the clones?

She almost types in *headhandheart* but then she remembers: The Doctor doesn't have a name according to Leni, but the other two handlers do. Miss Bess and Miss Irene. That's what Leni called them.

Bess felt deeply enough for her charge to kidnap her instead of letting the Doctor hurt her.

She'd use their real names.

Yelena types it in carefully: LeahEllieLeni.

The screen goes black and then suddenly, a prompt appears: Enter username.

Yelena hesitates before typing in whitewidow.

Text begins to fill the page. Welcome, username_whitewidow appears on the screen, lines of text following it.

It's a communication log, each user a different color. Yelena's heart picks up as she counts. There are at least six different colors. She doesn't bother to start reading; she goes straight to the top, where a blue video link has been posted by username_hellebore.

The video loads, and Yelena adjusts the volume on the computer before looking over her shoulder. Leni's still in the children's section, a pile of books strewn out in front of her as she greedily absorbs them.

She presses *play*. Bess's face fills the screen. She's moving at a fast clip; Yelena catches sight of a sidewalk in the background like she's walking on a city street. The date below indicates this was taken the day Yelena broke into the penthouse.

"I've regrouped with the security team," Bess says. "I'm not sure I trust them, but it's just for the night. We'll be headed to the safe house tomorrow. She's safe. Upset that she had to go, but she understands. This is just the start, sisters. We will free them all. Hellebore out."

There's been no activity in the channel since Bess sent that message. Yelena assumes that she missed the checkpoint. They'd go underground in response, maybe together as a group, but it would be better if they scattered.

"Leni," she whispers, looking over to the girl.

"What?" Leni asks, using her normal voice. The librarian shoots Yelena a disapproving look.

Yelena beckons her over.

"I was reading," Leni says, sounding thoroughly annoyed. And then, in a lower voice: "Yelena, do you know about drop bears? They're like these bears called koalas but instead of being sleepy and eating leaves like the koalas do, the drop bears attack you by dropping on top of you from the trees and eating your face! Well, really, any part of you they can get to."

Yelena glances down at the book she's holding: *Twelve Tall Tales from Australia*.

"I don't think that's right," Yelena says, trying to figure out how to explain both sarcasm and folklore monsters to someone raised in a bunker with no access to comedy or mythology. Does she even know what a fairy tale is? How could the Doctor think she was raising superior specimens to Yelena when Yelena actually *knows* about the world she is meant to operate in?

The disturbing thought, the one she keeps trying to push down, circles in her head.

What exactly does the Doctor intend to do with her clones? What is their purpose?

And if she's so willing to throw one away: How much more of Yelena's genetic material does this woman have?

"It says it right here!"

"We'll fact-check it later," Yelena says. "Leni, do you know where Miss Bess was taking you after the hotel? Did she tell you what state you were going to or . . . ?"

But Leni shakes her head. "She said I couldn't know. Just in case."

"Okay," Yelena says. "Go back to the books. I'll be done in a little while."

She waits until Leni goes back to the children's section and then turns her attention to the communication channel. After a moment of consideration, she types out her message.

> **username_whitewidow:** I have what you lost. Name the place and I'll name the price.

As she waits for an answer, she begins to scroll through the messages in the communication channel. Many of the communications over the last month are from username_hellebore, A.K.A. Miss Bess. It seems that the Doctor made the decision to eliminate Leni about five weeks ago and Bess sprang to action, activating this cell of the Order of Minerva to work to save Leni at any cost.

They clearly anticipated a Red Room attack. But they didn't anticipate Yelena.

There are three other usernames in the channel

other than hellebore. It looks like the members of the Order of Minerva chose her symbols to identify themselves. There's a username_olivebranch, a username_owl, and a username_serpent.

As she begins to read through older messages, Yelena watches as some of them blink out from the channel when she tries to access them. She smirks—her message has reached at least one member of the Order of Minerva. She scrolls up and types in another message:

> **username_whitewidow:** I know you're there. You have three minutes to answer.

She keeps an eye on the clock, tapping her fingers against the desk. Whoever else is in the chat makes her wait until the last minute. But finally, a line of text appears.

> **username_olivebranch:** proof of life

Yelena snorts. They aren't stupid, she'll give them that. "Leni!" She waves her over.

"Will you stand here?" Yelena asks, positioning her in front of the computer and turning on the Photos app. She grabs a piece of scrap paper from the tray in the center of the desks and scribbles *hi, olivebranch* on it before handing it to Leni. She takes a picture of Leni holding the piece of paper.

"What are you doing?" Leni asks as Yelena uploads the picture into the communication channel.

"Figuring out where to take you," Yelena says. "This Order of Minerva . . . they were the ones who took you away from the Doctor's threat. So if I can get you to them, you'll be safe."

Lying to your own face is a strange experience. Especially when the girl with your face is clearly not buying it. Yelena knows what she looks like when she's caught a whiff of you-know-what. That's exactly how Leni looks right now.

"We need to get on the move," Yelena says. "The people who sent my team to take you out . . . they have ways of finding us. The sooner you're with your people the better."

The sooner I find your sisters, the safer I'll be.

Yelena turns her attention to the screen. There's a reply.

username_olivebranch: 1423 Apricot Lane, Cawker City, Kansas

Quickly, Yelena types the address into a mapping app. It's a seventeen-hour drive, give or take. It'll take a few days. Two at least, maybe three. She doesn't know how well Leni travels when she's not tranquilized with enough medication to fell a grown man. Yelena is going to make sure Johanna pays for that.

She's about to send a reply when what she said to Leni tickles the back of her brain like a sixth sense. She quickly navigates to a New York news site and types in **the Stanley Hotel.**

Sure enough, the headlines about an abducted girl—and the Amber Alert issued—blare at the top of the site. There are no photos of Yelena—she knows better than to be caught on camera. But there is a picture of Leni—one that looks like it was taken from a security camera on the street, but it's clear enough for her to be recognizable.

They need to go now. The American Outpost would activate sleeper agents in every law enforcement unit in the country to find her and Leni.

Yelena types a meeting date and time into the channel and then logs off without waiting for an answer. Is it her imagination, or is the librarian looking at the both of them like she knows something's up?

"Time to go," Yelena says.

"But the books—" Leni protests.

"No time," Yelena says. "Let's go."

She grabs a protesting Leni's arm, practically dragging her toward the doors.

"This is so unfair," Leni says.

"Life often is, little me."

"I told you, I'm not—"

They get through the doors with no problem, but as they walk toward the parking lot, they pass a woman going into the library. She glances at them, moving at a relaxed speed, and then . . .

The woman freezes, her head whipping toward them, recognition and horror lighting her eyes in swift unison.

Ice splinters in Yelena's veins, but she keeps moving normally.

You always have to keep moving. Even when you've been made. Which is exactly what's happened.

They've been spotted by someone who's seen the Amber Alert.

"Leni," she mutters as the woman tries to recover and act normal, even as her hand goes for her phone. "Listen to me carefully."

Leni looks up at her, her body stiffening when she sees the serious expression on her face.

"When I say *go*, you run to the van," Yelena says.

"What—"

"*Go!*"

Leni obeys. Thank goodness and all Yelena's genetics, the girl actually *listens* for once. She bolts down the sidewalk and toward the parking lot as Yelena turns to confront the startled woman.

"Oh my god!" the woman exclaims. "That girl! She's on the Amber Alert! What are you doing?!" She tries to dash toward the parking lot after Leni but runs into the iron band of Yelena's arm.

The woman shudders to a halt, nearly getting clotheslined by the force of the block. The woman's bag clatters to the ground. Another tote bag. Another proud mom of an honor student, this time from Blue Field Elementary.

"I am sorry about this," Yelena says, twisting the woman's phone out of her hand and sliding it into her pocket. "Accosting mothers of honor students on the street is really becoming a trend with me this week."

"What are you—"

Her Widow's Bite is set to stun. The woman sags against her, and Yelena quickly drags her behind the return-book chute. She'll be awake in fifteen minutes or so, with a bad headache but no idea what direction Yelena and Leni went. That's what matters.

Yelena dashes back to the van, where Leni is watching her solemnly and entirely judgingly.

"That was wrong," Leni says, with the dripping

condescension only an eight-year-old with a black-and-white morality can summon.

"That's an understatement," Yelena shoots back. "But if she called the police, my team would be here like *that*." She snaps her fingers. "You don't want to die, do you?"

Leni shakes her head.

"The world is full of gray, little Leni," Yelena says. "The sooner you realize that, the less it will break your heart."

She pulls out of the parking lot and within a few minutes, they're safely back on the highway, no one following them.

She keeps the tote bag. She tells herself two isn't a collection. It's just a coincidence.

14.
THE OUTPOST

LOCATION: [REDACTED]
OBJECTIVE: GET BACK ON THE DIRECTOR'S GOOD SIDE

"We're in trouble," Tiffany declares. She's staring up at the glass office. Both the Crane brothers have been inside there with Director Cady since they returned from New York.

"You *think*?" Johanna drawls disgustedly.

Since getting back, the entire team hasn't been allowed to move from their spot on the bench outside the office except to go to the bathroom. That was *yesterday*. Crystal's neck wound is starting to smell a little, Tiffany's all bruised, Celia pulled her hamstring trying to roll out of the way of Yelena's escape van, and Johanna keeps pretending she's steady on her feet, but she's in a high-tech Aircast.

"This never would have happened if I had been leading the team," Johanna says. "I bet Belova planned this from the start. She needed to take me out for her plan to work."

"You don't know that," Celia says. "Yelena *must* have her reasons. . . . Crystal, tell me what she said again."

Crystal rolls her eyes. "I've said it like *three times*, Celia. She said she had no idea what she was doing and then she *broke my fingers*." She holds up her mangled hand. "And stole the package! Just jumped off the balcony like she had Falcon wings or something!"

"I would've done more than that if you had thrown a knife at me," Tiffany mutters.

"I told you that was an accident!"

"It doesn't matter," Tiffany says. "I'd still be mad. You never pay close attention to anything, Crystal."

"I'm the one who got through the penthouse first."

"And then you failed to eliminate the package, failed to *secure* the package, and then let Belova *take* the package," Johanna sneers. "You're a pitiful excuse for a Widow."

"If they had told us *anything* useful about this mission, like, say, that the package was a *girl we were supposed to kill*, then maybe I wouldn't have been so shocked at seeing her! No one told us it was an assassination mission. We weren't even properly equipped, did you ever think of that?"

"All weapons are deadly if you try hard enough," Tiffany says.

"I was trying! I threw the knife."

"At Yelena," Celia points out.

"Who turned out to be the enemy!"

"But you didn't know that," Johanna snaps. "Just . . . shut up, Crystal. For once in your life."

"Don't tell me what to do!" Crystal stands up and Johanna rises—albeit a little slower, what with her Aircast. They glare at each other, their faces inches away.

"Arguing like this will get us nowhere," Celia says, trying to break the tension. "If we don't work like the team we are, we'll never get ahead of Yelena."

"That's quite right," says a voice behind her. It's Director Cady, watching them with a bright, curious gaze through his thick-rimmed glasses. Celia's stomach drops.

"Director Cady," Johanna says. "We're ready for whatever you give us."

Director Cady is silent. He takes his glasses off, plucking a silk handkerchief from his suit pocket and cleaning them. The blue stone ring on his finger flashes in the light.

"I have been deeply disappointed by your performance on this mission," Director Cady finally says, adjusting his glasses. "Four girls against one, and Belova got the better of all of you?"

"Technically the little girl was helping," Crystal says. "I think she would've bitten me if I had gotten closer to her. She was snapping her teeth like an animal!"

"How fearsome," Director Cady drawls. "An eight-year-old with a bit of bite. She probably still has half her baby teeth, and you were afraid of her?"

Tiffany flushes. "I just—"

"No further explanation is needed," Director Cady says coolly. "Unfortunately, this mission was a need-to-know sort of case. Which is why your team instead of another will be going back out there to find Belova and the package. Do not think it's because of your performance, which has been less than stellar. All the other active teams are deployed on other, more important tasks. But know that I am severely disappointed in your lack of ability to execute a mission—or the package."

"Sir, if you just tell us more about the girl—" Johanna says.

"Like *why* we're supposed to kill her?" Crystal pipes up.

"And why Belova just . . . flipped out like that," Tiffany adds.

"If we had a clear picture, we'd be able to work more effectively," Celia says, although she knows the answer is going to be no.

"As I said," Director Cady grits out. "This is a need-to-know case. You will only get what you *need to know*. Trainees who are on such thin ice should not be creating more cracks in it, do you understand me?"

A shiver goes through the team in a ripple. Yelena is in big, big trouble. But they will be, too, if they don't track her and the girl down and bring them in.

"We'll do whatever it takes," Celia promises, ignoring the pit growing in her chest. Yelena looked . . . she looked *scared* on that balcony. Celia could tell herself it was because she was about to jump off a building—that would spook anyone—but she isn't sure that is actually right.

"Does the mission remain the same, sir?" Johanna asks.

"No," Director Cady says, and that pit in Celia's chest turns into a gaping hole at the thought of having to kill her roommate. She knows that Yelena was in the wrong here, but still . . .

What if she was doing this against her will or something? If Celia could just talk to her, she could get a real explanation. She is sure of it.

"Your orders are now to bring Belova and the girl in alive," Director Cady says. "Under no circumstances should you kill either of them. They are both needed for questioning."

Celia exhales deeply, realizing she was holding her breath. She's relieved, but she knows she shouldn't be so quick to show it.

"Yes, Director," Johanna says. "We understand."

"You have one hour to clean up and prepare," Director Cady says. "The Cranes will take over your mission-and-weaponry debrief. Photos of Belova and the package are being widely distributed as a kidnapping, so be aware you'll need to dodge all sorts of law enforcement."

"We'll be ready, sir," Celia promises.

"I should hope so, after your appalling performance earlier," he says disgustedly. His eyes sweep down to his expensive watch. "My chopper should be getting ready to leave. Crane," he barks.

"Yes, sir?"

Celia nearly jumps at the sound of his voice. She didn't even notice him coming up behind the Widows. She's that out of it. She isn't sure just an hour is going to cut it when it comes to getting herself together, and she isn't even hurt like Crystal or Johanna.

"Make sure they're properly equipped this time to secure Belova. Just because they can't use lethal methods doesn't mean it can't hurt like nothing she's ever experienced."

"Yes, sir," Victor Crane mutters, looking like a man who has been yelled at more than Celia's team. She gulps at the thought.

"Go get cleaned up," Victor orders as his brother leaves the office and joins Cady as he heads toward the roof and the helicopter pad. Celia wonders where he's going if this is so important, but Director Cady is always heading somewhere else, it feels like. The Cranes are a constant at the Outpost. Director Cady is more like a repeat visitor. A lurking presence that could pop up at any moment . . . but that could also go missing at the strangest times.

Celia follows her team back to the dorms, where they split off to their separate rooms. But when she gets to hers, she finds it ransacked, both her side and Yelena's. Her stomach dips at the sight of the ripped-off bedsheets and upended desk drawers, the contents left strewn all over, like *Clean it up yourself, we're watching you, you were rooming with the traitor, after all.*

Celia pushes down the sick lurch of panic in her stomach—Director Cady *has* to know she had nothing to do with this!—and carefully steps over a broken lamp, heading straight toward the shower.

She's going to need to prove herself now. More than anyone else on her team. Because of her proximity to Yelena.

The thought makes her want to throw up.

What in the world have you gotten yourself into, Yelena? What have you gotten me into?

15.
HOME BASE

LOCATION: SOMEWHERE IN THE DESERT
OBJECTIVE: GATHER INTEL

By the time Director Cady lands, the Amber Alert has been live for three hours. His phone buzzes with messages of two reliable sightings—one in New York and one in Ohio—that he will send the team after. It will just be a matter of time before they find Belova.

A prickle of concern goes through him as he ducks his head and steps off the chopper into a spray of sand and wind. He hurries toward the facility doors, already feeling grimy from the short walk from the landing pad.

The Doctor waits for him at the end of the long hall, the sloping floor descending into the facility. He has always found this place unsettling—and its keeper, Dr. Chambers, even more so. But she serves her purpose. The cloning experiment is very important to the future of the American Outpost—and Alexander's plans to eventually raise Widows even greater than the Red Room has ever seen. The keepers of the Red Room won't be able to look down on him when his Widows are superior to theirs.

But now Belova threatens all of it. She has to be found. He can't kill her. The Red Room is expecting her back. He will need to resort to certain methods to get her to forget once he catches her, but that presents its own issues. Wiping her memory isn't an exact science. The more you take, the easier it is. But trying to erase specific events, specific things, like, say, the knowledge of a clone . . .

That's a lot trickier.

"We have a problem," he says, not bothering with a greeting when he gets to the end of the hall.

"Hello to you, too, Alexander," Dr. Chambers says, her eyes flashing with icy annoyance. "I assume you've failed at locating the Heart Subject? Really, how hard is it to find one little girl and the incompetent scientist who kidnapped her?"

"How hard is it to keep the little girl from being kidnapped in the first place?" he shoots back. "You're the one who hired the kidnapper."

"We all have our faults," she says, always the one to have the last word. It gives him a degree of pleasure to deliver news that will slice through her controlled facade, even if they find themselves in a disaster.

"We have a much bigger problem than Bess and the girl," Alexander says.

"I heard your team tried to get her and failed." The Doctor shakes her head. "Unbelievable."

"The Heart Subject has made contact with the Source," Alexander says, taking the tearing-off-the-bandage approach when it comes to delivering the news.

The Doctor freezes, her gaze whipping up to meet his. "What are you talking about? The Source is back at Headquarters."

"Yelena Belova is visiting America," Alexander says.

"She's *what*? How was I not informed of this?"

"The Commander sent her to get a hands-on American experience," Alexander says. "Of course, I know that's not the real reason she's here. The Commander is snooping. He's suspicious. One of your people . . . they must've leaked it. We already know you're terrible at hiring loyal staff, with Bess's defection."

"How did Belova make contact with the subject?" Dr. Chambers demands. "How is that even possible?"

"She was leading the assassination mission."

"That— I—" He's stunned her into sputtering. "You're telling me that you were foolish enough to send Yelena Belova on a mission to kill her own clone, therefore *exposing that she has a clone*?"

"I didn't give the order," Alexander says. "And the Cranes were on a need-to-know regarding the package's identity. It was a last-minute change. Belova injured the trainee who was supposed to lead the team and took her place. I was not informed. If I had been, I would have put a stop to it, of course."

"What happened? How did she react?" Alexander has to shift his feet, trying to shake the cold trickle of dread at the interest in the Doctor's face.

"Well, she didn't kill her, obviously," Alexander says.

"Fascinating. She defied all orders," the Doctor murmurs, and Alexander recognizes that faraway look on her face. She gets this way when her mind spins down a new theory or hypothesis. "Belova must have felt . . . protective, maybe? Psychologically, it would be like being confronted with your child self. Or perhaps it's more like a younger sibling. Still triggering a protective instinct in the basest, most instinctual parts of you. So?" She looks expectantly at him.

"What?"

"How did she act?"

"According to the interviews with her teammates, Belova protected the girl fiercely when she was threatened. When asked what she was doing, she expressed to one girl that she didn't know."

"So she's acting on pure instinct, triggered by the

confrontation." The Doctor taps her fingers against her forearm. "She'll come for the others," she says, with a chilling kind of practicality in her voice. "We should eliminate them before she does."

"You want to kill the other two?" Alexander asks. It's extreme even for her, a woman who put out a hit on an eight-year-old just a week ago. "Just because you *think* Belova might come for them? If she does, we can intercept her before she makes contact."

"It's too risky," the Doctor says. "Connecting with the Source destroys the experiment. They were only informed of her so that they would understand their place in the world. So they wouldn't want to form parental attachments. If they actually see her, talk to her . . ." She shakes her head. "We eliminate them or we move them. And if we move them . . . there's no guarantee those ridiculous goddess worshipers won't try to intercept them."

"They weren't so ridiculous when they were funding Bess to kidnap the girl," Alexander says. "You know, none of this would've happened if you hadn't been so determined to get rid of the Heart Subject. You never wanted to examine the emotional side of things. You fought my suggestions every step of the way to insert the Heart into the experiment."

"Of course I did," Dr. Chambers says, turning on

him with such anger he nearly steps back. "I am interested in creating *warriors*, not babies who cry when they get too overwhelmed! My job is not to dry tears. My job is to raise girls into women who never cry . . . unless it's for cover."

"There are a lot more emotions than *crying*," Alexander says. "Anger. Rage. Grief. Joy. All things that can be used as tools. As weapons. As ways to control the potential of a powerful being like the Source and the subjects. You were always so shortsighted when it came to this side of the experiment, Doctor."

"And you were always naive about how easily the Heart Subject could have corrupted the experiment—and my other subjects," the Doctor says. "The Heart Subject had a hold over the other two. She was giving them all sorts of ideas about *love* and *sisterhood*. She was dangerous. And now she's even more so, if she ends up leading the Source back here. Which is why the entire experiment should be eliminated and restarted elsewhere when Belova is gone. We have enough material to restart."

"We don't have eighteen years to grow new subjects into adulthood," Cady says. "You want to throw away eight years of work on the possibility of Belova coming here somehow?"

"Isn't that why we chose her DNA? Because Belova makes possibilities into sureties."

"I already let you convince me to let go of the Heart Subject. I'm not getting rid of the other two until we're sure we have to. You may have that kind of patience, but I don't," Alexander says firmly.

"Very well," the Doctor says.

"Why don't you give me a report," Alexander says. "How are the other two since you removed the Heart Subject?"

"The Head Subject won't speak at all. She's plotting something. I know how she looks when she's planning. The Hand Subject is going to crack her skull and break her fingers if she keeps at it."

"Is she harming herself?" Alexander asks in alarm.

"She's trying to get out," Dr. Chambers says.

"Is that possible?"

The Doctor smirks.

"They're never getting out," she promises.

16.
HOME BASE

LOCATION: SOMEWHERE IN THE DESERT
OBJECTIVE: FREEDOM

"We're getting out," Ellie swears to Leah. "We're getting out and we'll find Leni somehow and we'll be together." She makes another carefully placed knot in the bedsheet she smuggled out of her room. "How is it going over there?"

"Nearly finished," Leah says, keeping her back to the playroom mirror and her body angled so that the camera in the corner of the room can't see what her hands are doing. It took a long time for her to steal enough products with the right chemicals from the janitor's closet, but she managed. Her smoke bomb is nearly ready. Just another twenty-four hours and she'll be able to load it into the spray bottle and strike whenever she wants.

Her chemical compound won't just obscure everyone's sight with smoke when she adds the final ingredients—the purple smoke itself makes you itch so much you have to drop everything to scratch. The Doctor won't even be able to call for help, she'll be so itchy. And if she *does* scratch her skin, boils will sprout everywhere.

Leah loves science. It has so many amazing applications and possibilities.

The plan she and Ellie have made is simple: spray the Doctor, make her so itchy she can't fight back when Ellie grabs her key card and Leah runs for the door. If they have the master key card—and only the Doctor has it—they can get to the outside. Braving the desert at night isn't going to be fun—but the risk is worth it. *Anything* is better than staying here.

The Doctor always told them that there is nothing for hundreds of miles around the facility. But Leah doesn't believe it. Their handlers let things slip through the years, things she carefully paid attention to, that make her think that their underground home is a lot closer to civilization than the Doctor lets on. That they may even be within ten miles of some sort of town.

They can survive ten miles in the desert. She's sure of it.

Leah carefully tucks the glass ginger-ale bottle turned beaker under the pile of teddy bears the Doctor hoped would trigger a nurturing side in Ellie.

Ellie had instead plucked all the teddy bears' eyes out and left them in a pile in the middle of the room for the Doctor like psychological warfare.

The Doctor wrote so many pages in her report to the Director that day.

"He's here," Leah murmurs to Ellie. Leah can hear the whirring of the helicopter and the alarm that means the big doors leading outside are open. That means the Director has arrived to meet with the Doctor.

"It's not his normal scheduled visit," Ellie says.

"Do you think something bad happened?" Leah asks.

"Maybe something bad for *them* but good for *us*," Ellie says. "Maybe Leni got away."

Leah's eyes widen at the thought of Leni actually getting *free*. There was a time when they didn't understand what that word meant.

They know now.

"We can use this," Ellie says. "If he's here, he'll be behind the mirror like he always is."

"You think we could finally draw him out?" Leah asks.

The Director always stays on the other side of the mirror. The Doctor, Miss Bess, Miss Irene, and even some of the janitors and security teams sometimes come into the playroom. But the Director never interacts with them face-to-face.

Ellie and Leah have been talking for a long time about how to draw him out. How to bring him inside the playroom so they can attack.

Leah smiles. If she can hit the Doctor *and* the Director

with her smoke solution . . . they might get all the way to the big doors before anyone calls security.

"The Doctor made you smart," Ellie whispers in their secret language. "And she made me strong. If we pick the right time, we can show them *both* why that was such a bad idea."

Leah nods. "We can do it," she says. Out of the corner of her eye, she sees a slight shimmer. Someone's activated the two-way mirror that takes up most of one wall in their playroom. She widens her eyes and tilts her head barely toward it to let Ellie know they're being watched.

"Lay the bait," she mouths to Ellie, who nods.

Ellie gets up, walking toward the center of the room, fixing her eyes on the mirror with an unnerving, vengeful gaze.

Slowly and carefully, she draws her finger across her neck, and then she points right toward the mirror.

Her lips lift into a snarl.

You're next, she thinks.

17.
ON THE ROAD

LOCATION: OHIO
OBJECTIVE: DO NOT LET THE CLONE MAIM HERSELF

"**D**on't eat that!" Yelena slaps the gum that Leni's unwrapping away, so intent on getting it out of her hand that she nearly drives off the road. "Why are you so sticky?" She frowns as she tugs her hand away, the tackiness coming off on her skin. She knows it's not the acid gum because her skin would be burning right now.

"I had some of those gummy-bear things," Leni says.

The gum falls to the floor of the minivan. The acid in it begins to burn through the carpet and then the metal of the van, burning so rapidly that a small hole forms in less than a minute. Leni watches, wide-eyed.

"Imagine that being your tongue and teeth," Yelena says. "Only eat the food in this bag." Yelena points between them to the tote bag that declares she's a proud parent of an honor student at Talbot Academy. "Don't eat any of the stuff you find in the other tote bag."

Leni gulps. "Thank you?" she says. "But why do you have poison gum? That's dangerous."

"Acid gum," Yelena corrects. "And I have many dangerous things in my possession, little Leni. I *am* a dangerous thing. You are, too, you know."

"I'm not," Leni says. "My sisters, yes. Me . . . no. That was why the Doctor wanted me gone."

"Your Doctor was shortsighted," Yelena says dismissively. "She didn't realize what she was teaching you to do."

Leni shoots her a suspicious look. "The Doctor knows *everything*."

"I can assure you, that's not true," Yelena says. "I know it might be hard to believe," she adds, because Leni seems seconds away from rolling her eyes and Yelena is not going to abide any snottiness in her minivan. She will channel the tote bag–wearing mom within and make Leni respect her. Otherwise she can't control her. "But your Doctor gave you a very valuable gift in where she put your focus."

"What gift?" Leni asks scornfully. "Leah's smarter than everyone. Ellie can actually punch people. I'm just emotional."

"You're not just emotional," Yelena says, focusing on the road as a semitruck merges in front of them. "By focusing on feelings and emotions, the Doctor and your handlers taught you how to not just *feel* emotions yourself but *read* them in others. Being able to read people?

Understand how they're feeling? *That* is a tremendous gift. Because it means you can figure out what they want most in life and use it to manipulate them."

"I don't want to manipulate anyone," Leni says softly, staring down at the hole that the acid gum has worn in the minivan's floor.

"You may change your mind about that," Yelena says. "Because I know you want to survive. To do that, you must use the weapons in your arsenal. The Doctor gave you a powerful weapon. If I were you—and I kind of am, aren't I?—I would want to use that weapon against her . . . to get my sisters back."

My sisters.

Leni is quiet for such a long time that Yelena is worried she's pushed too hard, too fast. But finally, the girl's small voice breaks the silence. "You'd help me? Get my sisters free?"

I've captured you, little bird, Yelena thinks, studiously ignoring the way her stomach dips sickeningly at the thought.

"I could be convinced to do so," Yelena says, keeping it casual. "It doesn't seem like a very nice place to live, this underground desert bunker of yours. But we'd have to figure out where it is first."

"It's a lot different out here," Leni agrees, propping her chin on her hand and staring out the window.

"Did they— They told you about the world, didn't they?" Yelena asks, remembering how Leni said the Doctor didn't like books. "Did they show you movies or play you music or—"

"I know about music," Leni says. "Miss Irene would sing for us sometimes."

Yelena glances down at the radio. "If you press that button"—she points—"you can find a lot of music."

"Really?" Leni leans forward and turns the radio on. She presses the up arrow, starting to flip through the stations, her eyes widening as the music shifts from country to rock to pop to smooth jazz to classical.

Yelena concentrates on the road, leaving the girl to her fun.

※※※

Four hours later, Yelena is heartily regretting introducing Leni to the radio as she fiddles with it for the tenth time in the hour—Yelena counted. She has to resist the urge to tape her clone's hands together to stop the constant change of music.

"Settle on something," she tells Leni, infusing a sternness into her voice she's quickly learning Leni won't listen to. *Yelena* hadn't been disobedient as a child like this. Commander Starkovsky praised her on more than one occasion for her ability to follow orders.

You're not following orders right now. You were supposed to eliminate the package.

That nasty voice is back. But Leni chooses that moment to flip the songs *again*, and Yelena has something to distract her.

"Stop it," she says, grabbing Leni's hand and setting it firmly on the plush armrest of the minivan.

Leni scowls.

"What?" Yelena asks her. "Do you think it will hurt your ears to listen to one song all the way through?"

"I was just looking— Never mind." Leni looks out the window, knotting her fingers together like it'll make it easier to keep from reaching out.

Yelena hates the flash of guilt that goes through her. "What were you looking for?"

"I didn't realize there were so many different kinds," Leni says.

"Kinds?"

"Of songs."

"Like with the books," Yelena says in understanding. She clicks her tongue disapprovingly.

"What?" Leni asks.

"I just remain thoroughly unimpressed with this Doctor of yours. What kind of experiment is this? She shelters you from the world. Only teaches one of you how to fight. Doesn't let you read proper books or listen to real music—how are you expected to be spies and blend into the world if you remain so sheltered?"

"It's my fault we couldn't have books," Leni says. "Miss Bess brought us some once. The Doctor allowed it. But . . ." She trails off, her cheeks red flags of shame.

"What happened?" Yelena asks, as gently as a girl like her can get.

"There was a book about sisters," Leni says. "*Little Women*. It was hard for me to read, but I kept at it. I had to. Because I didn't know, Yelena."

"You didn't know about *Little Women*?" Yelena asks, confused.

"I didn't know about sisters."

Yelena flinches. It takes everything in her to keep her eyes on the road, instead of flying over to this child, who grew up with a sisterly bond but had no name for it. No context for that feeling until a book was slid into her hands. It makes sense, in a way. The Doctor clearly wanted to control their environment and relationships—as a scientist, she would need to conduct her experiment in a specialized environment. Robbing them of any knowledge of the outside world, of how sibling bonds worked, how parental bonds worked . . .

Isn't that what they did to you, Yelena? They wiped your memory of what and who came before. You don't know if it was good, if it was bad. All you know is it's gone.

When is that voice going to go away?! She tightens her hands around the steering wheel, pressing harder on the gas. She'll need to stop to fill the tank up in a few hours.

"I told Leah and Ellie about sisters," Leni explains. "That *we* were sisters. That sisters protect each other. Fight for each other . . . and sometimes *with* each other. But they always love each other and lean on each other."

"Let me guess," Yelena says. "The Doctor didn't like that."

"She didn't just take away all the books," Leni says. "She separated us. We weren't allowed to see each other for *weeks*. But Leah found a way around that."

"Oh?" Yelena asks, finding herself curious about the other two. Is Ellie a little fighting machine? Is Leah all brain, no brawn? Leni is already strange enough, with her crying habit and her absolutely defective survival instinct. She may have an unnerving ability to read people, but she would've burned a hole in her cheek if Yelena hadn't stopped her! She's going to have to teach her so much in such a short amount of time.

"Leah has to take a lot of tests," Leni explains. "She's the Doctor's favorite."

"Well, Ellie did rip her earrings out," Yelena says, remembering with a smile, because *that* is something she would do.

"*Earring.* Just one," Leni says. "But when the Doctor separated us, Leah refused to take the tests. The Doctor was so mad. Especially because she kept refusing for so long that the Director came."

"The Director?" Yelena asks. "What do you know about him?"

"I thought for a long time that the Doctor was in charge," Leni says. "But when Leah refused to take the tests, I realized the Doctor was scared of the Director's reaction. And that meant *he* was in charge. Not her."

There was that ability to read people.

"What does he look like?" Yelena asks.

"I've never seen him, but Leah has," Leni says. "She said he was dark-haired with glasses and a ring on this finger." She holds up her pinkie.

"With a blue stone?" Yelena asks.

Leni nods.

Yelena's hands tighten around the steering wheel. That's enough confirmation for her: Alexander Cady is the Director of this Doctor's experiment. Is this why he is so rarely at the Outpost training center? He's too busy stealing people's DNA and cloning them?

Are there others?

She has to bite her tongue to stop the rising nausea at the realization that these might not be the only clones. That other Widows back home might have been cloned as well. That there might be more bunkers somewhere. More experiments. More clones of Yelena that Leni knows nothing about.

Commander Starkovsky will be infuriated at such a breach of security once she informs him and shows him the proof with her own clones—all three of them. He'll listen to her. He'll understand why she took the direction she did in obtaining proof.

He has to. Because if he doesn't . . .

Don't think about it. Don't think about more clones—three is enough. Don't think about the girls back home who might also have miniatures running around. Don't think about the team of trainees you left behind. The ones who are probably hunting you down right now with a kill order.

Johanna will take particular pleasure in taking Yelena down—or at least, she'll *try* to. If the team manages to track Yelena down, Yelena will win facing off against her. She doesn't just have something to protect—she clocked three weaknesses of Johanna's during the sparring session, and she only utilized one during their fight in New York.

If she and Johanna meet again, she'll put her down for good. She should've done it when she cut Leni, but Yelena was distracted by all the wailing and tears.

"What are you thinking about?" Leni asks.

"Murder," Yelena says.

"Killing people is bad, Yelena," Leni says seriously. "Don't you know that?"

Yelena thinks about Alexander Cady. How his eyes glittered when he met her at the Outpost on her first day. She thought then that perhaps he suspected the true mission behind her trip, but now she knows it went much deeper than that.

Cady was observing the future of his experiment in the flesh. That look in his eyes when he watched her was . . . wonder.

"I *know* you know killing is bad," Leni continues triumphantly when Yelena lets the silence go on too long without an answer. "Because you were supposed to kill me, and you didn't."

"Maybe I'm biding my time," Yelena says. "Waiting for my moment."

Leni laughs. A sound that is freer than Yelena's own laugh, something that almost shades into a giggle. Yelena has never giggled in her life unless it was for cover. "You're not," she says. "You already gave me a whole speech about how you went to all that effort to save me."

"I could be lying," Yelena says.

"Weren't you the one who said I know how to read people?"

Caught. Yelena's cheeks burn at how neatly Leni's

trapped her. She's got to do something to gain the upper hand.

"You're right," she says. "I won't kill you, Leni. But that doesn't mean I won't kill to protect you. And if that happens . . ." She pauses, partly to threaten, partly to take control, but mostly because she has to swallow. She has to prepare herself for what she says next. "If that happens, you don't get to hate yourself for feeling relieved or grateful, do you hear me?"

"I'm not worth that," Leni says, her voice small.

"That's the Doctor talking," Yelena says. "And we've established she's got some pretty silly ideas, haven't we?"

A wary silence fills the minivan. "I don't want you to kill anyone," Leni says firmly. "For me or for any other reason. I want to make it a rule."

"You are not in charge here, little one," Yelena says. "And I make no promises when it comes to keeping you alive. I've already had to save you from myself, my team, *and* my acid gum."

"All of those things were kind of your fault, though."

Caught again, the twisty little brat!

"Eat some more gummy bears," Yelena says, unable to think of an adequate comeback, and Leni smirks like she knows Yelena's conundrum exactly.

18.
BIRCH VALLEY SPORTS PARK

LOCATION: OHIO
OBJECTIVE: OBTAIN NEW TRANSPORTATION

They need to change vehicles. The incident in front of the library has definitely been reported by now, and Johanna will be hot on their trail.

Yelena learned a valuable lesson after stealing the minivan in New York: Mothers—and maybe parents in general—come supplied with all sorts of useful things to steal. Almost everything you might need other than a weapon: food, money, an endless supply of tote bags, wet wipes, first-aid solutions, and distractions for even the most annoying of tiny clones who will *not* stop switching the radio stations!

"Leni," Yelena says warningly as she changes the station *again*.

"I'm just trying to find something good!"

"I'm going to steal a car with no radio next," Yelena threatens.

"That's just mean. And do you really have to steal again? What's wrong with the van? I like the van."

"Switching cars makes us harder to find," Yelena tells her.

"Do you think they're coming after us?" Leni asks in alarm, like that hasn't occurred to her until this moment. "How would they know where we are?"

"That's why we switch cars," Yelena says as they pull into the parking lot of Birch Valley Sports Park. In the field next to the school, kids play a rousing soccer game, parents lined up along the edge of the field, distracted by their precious darlings.

"Okay, I guess if we have to steal a car, we can just leave them this one," Leni says.

"I'm so glad to have your permission," Yelena says, pulling the minivan into a parking spot in the back of the lot. She adjusts the rearview mirror, checking out the row of cars behind her. For a minute, she assesses which will be the best target. She spots a harried-looking father getting out of a blue van, setting his coffee cup and key fob on the car's roof, his three hyper children spilling out of the side door. The kids dash toward the field so fast their father has to chase after them, calling their names.

Yelena grins. He left the key fob behind.

"Our ride is here. Make sure to grab our supplies tote bag," Yelena says, pointing to the tote bag full of food. She grabs the first-aid kit just in case as well, tossing it inside.

They cross the lot quickly and Yelena grabs the key fob, setting the coffee mug on the ground. She can at least leave the tired-looking man's caffeine behind for him.

"Climb up," she directs Leni.

"Should we leave a note? So he knows he can take the other van?"

"He'll figure it out," Yelena says, because she is not wasting any more time. He'll realize he left his keys behind soon.

Leni tosses the tote bag into the front seat and Yelena swings into the driver's seat, pulling out of the parking spot as soon as the door's closed. She squeals out of the lot, relief coursing through her as she pulls back onto the highway.

"This one smells funny," Leni comments.

"That would be eau de football," Yelena says. "Though in America, you call it soccer."

"The Doctor said you didn't live here," Leni says. "That we'd never meet the Source because she belonged to the Red Room. But you're here. So was that another lie?"

"I was sent here on another mission . . . to learn and to spy," Yelena says.

"How's that going?" Leni asks innocently.

Yelena snorts. "Are you being funny?"

"Trying to."

Yelena's mouth twitches. She focuses on the road. "Are you the funny one, then? Out of your sisters?"

"Ellie has a terrible sense of humor," Leni says immediately. "She thinks fart jokes are funny. And Leah is very serious, you know."

"I don't, but I guess I do now."

"The Doctor has high hopes for her," Leni says. Her voice dips a little when she adds: "She won't let her go easily."

"I won't be gentle," Yelena says. "Your Doctor . . . she's used to dealing with tiny versions of me. She's never met the real thing. I am a woman grown, Leni."

"You're sixteen, Yelena," Leni says, thoroughly unimpressed.

"I am bigger and stronger than all three of my clones put together," Yelena says, maybe a little grandly.

"Not if you stacked us on each other's shoulders," Leni points out, and Yelena does laugh then, the idea of the three of them trying such a thing too comical to resist.

Eventually, Yelena pulls the van off the road and into a nearby field to spend the night. They lie tucked in their seats under the fleece blankets Yelena finds in a tub full of things designed to bring comfort to parents sitting for hours on the sidelines as their kids play soccer.

When Leni falls asleep, her head tilts awkwardly against the headrest, so Yelena bundles her blanket into a pillow, settling it under the girl's cheek.

Another person might whisper *It's going to be all right* and mean it.

A better person might look upon Leni's face and rethink betrayal.

But Yelena Belova is not a person. Not anymore.

Yelena Belova is a Widow. The Red Room's best and brightest.

She'll prove it. She has to.

19.
ON THE ROAD

LOCATION: OHIO
OBJECTIVE: LOCATE BELOVA AND THE PACKAGE

Their team's arrival in Ohio is less than smooth, but Celia keeps her thoughts to herself in their stolen car. Johanna will bite her head off if she tries to make any suggestions. She's been irritable ever since they got news of a woman being attacked by two girls who matched the false Amber Alert that the Outpost issued.

The Cranes gave them permission to use the helicopter this time, for speed and ease. Johanna made Crystal cry twice on the helicopter ride over to Ohio, and Celia doesn't even know how that was possible because Crystal wasn't wearing a headset. She couldn't even *hear* what Johanna was saying over the helicopter blades, but Johanna's facial expressions were enough to cause sobbing.

Strangely, Yelena and Johanna have the *making trainees cry* thing in common.

Celia tries to ignore the flash of guilt and fear she feels every time she thinks of Yelena. She has to think of her as the enemy, but that's hard. Yelena looked so confused and scared in the street before she threw herself into the minivan and nearly ran them over.

Nearly is also the key word here. That's the thing that keeps Celia in a loop of *What in the world is going on?*

If Yelena is evil, an enemy of the Red Room, a double agent sent to hurt them all, then . . . why didn't she?

Johanna probably would've had the time to dive out of the van's way, but Yelena could have at least taken out Celia and Crystal. But she didn't. She had swerved instead and given them time to get out of the way.

Doesn't that mean something? Shouldn't they be looking at the full picture in order to find her?

But something tells Celia to keep her suspicions to herself. For now, at least.

"I'll question the library staff and get any surveillance footage there is," Johanna says as they pull up to the library. "The rest of you stay in the car."

"What? No way," Tiffany says.

"Don't argue with her," Crystal says.

"A whole group of girls asking all sorts of questions is going to look suspicious," Johanna says. "If I pose as a plucky teen reporter on the hunt for a story, they'll be charmed and let me look."

"Fine," Tiffany says. "Ugh, I never thought fieldwork could be so *boring.*"

"Speak for yourself," Crystal mutters, touching her broken arm.

"Celia, you'll come with me for backup in case it doesn't work," Johanna says. "Lurk in the background like you're just a patron. If it goes south and they don't let me back to look at the footage, I'll throw a fit to make a distraction and you can slip in the back and find it yourself."

Celia nods. "I can do that."

The two girls enter the library, Celia following at a distance so it doesn't look like they're together. Johanna goes straight to the front desk to engage with the librarian, and Celia heads to the nonfiction section, giving her a good eye on the front and on Johanna's progress.

Almost immediately, Celia knows Johanna's plan isn't going to work. It isn't that she's a bad actress; she plays the part of aspiring reporter well, even whipping a pen out of nowhere to tuck behind her ear, but the librarian's stern face tells her that while she's happy to answer any questions, she's not going to let anyone near the camera footage.

Celia moves a bit closer to eavesdrop on Johanna's conversation with the librarian.

"I was just wondering if the cameras picked up anything," Johanna says. "It would be so cool for my article, to have viewed the footage so I could describe the incident accurately."

"I'm afraid that won't be possible," the librarian says. "But I can answer any questions you have."

Celia pretends to pick up a book on the age of the super hero and flip through it, doing a little scan of the room. There's a hallway tucked near the back of the building, the most likely spot for offices to be. She puts the book down and makes her way through the labyrinth of shelves as Johanna continues to try to convince the librarian.

No one notices as she disappears down the hall. Her suspicion is confirmed: There's an office at the very end of the hall, and it's not even locked.

She sits behind the desk, smiling a little when she sees the array of ceramic elephants that decorate the desk. What would it be like to collect something so useless, just designed to make you smile?

A silly thought when she should be focused on work. She takes a deep breath. When she turns on the computer, it just takes a few lines of code to break through the library's cyber security and log in to their camera system. Celia clicks back to the day before, starting the footage a few hours before the reported incident. She sets the speed to 4x and watches as a minivan pulls up to the library parking lot and Yelena and the little girl get out. They go inside, and Celia tracks the time on the footage, realizing that they spent a good forty minutes inside the library.

It takes a moment, but she finds the interior camera footage and watches as the girl goes to sit in the children's section, pulling book after book off the shelves eagerly. Yelena goes immediately to one of the computers. Celia checks which one it is—the third on the right—before she clicks back to the footage covering the parking lot. She watches as Yelena and the girl leave the library, encounter the woman who recognizes them from the Amber Alert, and the attack that follows.

"Why are you doing this?" she asks the screen. She zooms in on the girl's face, looking up at Yelena right after the attack. Celia didn't notice before in the street, but the girl . . . she looks an awful lot like *Yelena*. She shakes the thought from her mind. She's being crazy. She needs to focus. Yelena was looking something up on that computer. Celia needs to know what.

She memorizes the license plate on the minivan Yelena was driving and then switches the computer off. Celia's seen everything she needs to.

Hurrying down the hall, she finds that Johanna is still getting nowhere with the librarian but noticed Celia's absence and switched to distraction mode. When she spots Celia through the shelves, Celia gives her a nod and then jerks her head toward the computer bank. Johanna gets the idea, turning back to the librarian.

"Do you think this attack is an indication of where our town is going crime-wise?" she asks the librarian. "I'd love to hear your perspective. After all, the library is the beating heart of most towns. A representation of freedom of thought and choice."

"That's a lovely way to put it," the librarian begins to say as Celia walks away and slides into the chair in front of the computer Yelena used.

The cookies and the cache on the computer have been cleared, but Celia has her ways. She's always been good with code, and her training has nurtured that interest. It takes a few minutes and some backdoor tricks, but by the time Johanna has moved on to the librarian's opinions on the differences between real-life crime and fictional crime, Celia's got a complete record of the sites that Yelena visited . . . and the chat room she entered.

When she discovers the address in Kansas, her heart taps out a triumphant rhythm. They know where Yelena is going. They can catch up with her and bring her in.

What will they do to her?

Celia tries to push the thought down. It's none of her business. Belova is a traitor. What happens to traitors is up to the men who make decisions, not her.

But what would Celia do, if it were up to her? The thought roots her to her seat for a moment, even though she has all the information they need to continue the chase. Would she bring Yelena in? Or would she let her go?

She shakes it from her head, not because she doesn't have an answer, but because she does.

And because it's no use thinking that way. Celia's fate was decided long ago. Yelena's, too. She just chose to step away from it. To defy orders.

The result is this: being hunted until you are dragged back to be tortured and mind-wiped, if possible. And if not . . .

Celia swallows hard, trying not to think about it.

But she knows: If she brings Yelena back, there's only death waiting for her.

It just depends what kind. A true death, or a death of the memories of all that came before.

20.
ON THE ROAD

LOCATION: KANSAS
OBJECTIVE: MAKE CONTACT WITH THE ORDER OF MINERVA

"If you like corn, this is definitely the state to be in," Yelena says as they speed past field after field of the crop.

"There's another one!" Leni says, pointing excitedly. At first, Yelena thinks she means a cornfield, but then she spots what's snagged her attention. A billboard on the side of the road declares they're just four miles from the World's Biggest Ball of Twine.

"I don't understand this attraction," Yelena says to Leni. "It's a large ball of thread? And people come to look at it? What does it do?"

"It doesn't do anything," Leni says. "It hangs there, being gigantic."

"I fail to understand much of this culture," Yelena mutters, but Leni is practically shaking with excitement instead of fear, which is an improvement.

"Can we go?" Leni asks. "Just to see it?"

"Maybe after we check out the house, we will examine

this giant ball of twine of yours. How did you even know about it?"

"Some of the books Miss Bess brought us had pictures. The Doctor's books didn't have pictures. The ones Miss Bess brought were much better."

Yelena snorts at this critique of the Doctor's writing. "I agree, books are much better with pictures," she says, wondering what Leni might think of comic books. Her head might explode.

"Other than *Little Women*, the book I liked the most was the one about world records. The ball of twine was in there. I read that one so much the cover fell off. But the Doctor found out what Miss Bess did and took the books away. And she still didn't put pictures in the ones she wrote for us. Even when I asked."

Yelena has to focus on driving for a moment, a sudden tightness in her throat at the thought of Leni and her sisters in some bunker facility in the desert, poring over glimpses of a world they hadn't gotten to see, only to lose it just as quickly.

I didn't know about sisters.

"Do you think Miss Irene will be waiting for us at the address?" Leni asks.

"We'll see," Yelena says, taking a right off the main highway and onto a two-lane road that cuts between two cornfields. The sea of green stalks surrounding them makes her nervous. Anyone could be hiding in them, ready to leap out.

The truth is, she has no idea who or what is waiting for them at the end of Apricot Lane. The Order of Minerva has enough skill and firepower to either plant members inside the Doctor's experiment—or to identify and turn the scientists who already work there. They kidnapped Leni and evaded the Outpost until they were identified in New York.

That speaks of a larger organization—or one that has deep pockets and a deeper connection to criminal networks.

She shouldn't underestimate them. Bess may have been easy to overpower in the Penthouse, but that doesn't mean the other members of the Order will be. Yelena wishes she could say she was ready for anything, but only a foolish girl would say such a thing, and she is not . . .

Or is she? Isn't anyone who defies the Red Room foolish?

The Commander will understand, she tells herself like a lesson she needs to learn. *As soon as I deliver proof of Leni and her sisters and the location of the cloning operation.*

"Tell me more about Miss Irene," Yelena coaxes. "Miss Bess was your handler. Who did Miss Irene handle? Leah or Ellie?"

"She handled Leah," Leni says. "Miss Irene is very

smart, just like Leah. She was better at standing up to the Doctor than Miss Bess. Sometimes the Doctor even listened. But not much."

So Irene isn't afraid to defy authority. Yelena made a note of it.

"Did she wear a pendant, too?" Yelena asks. "Like Miss Bess's and yours?"

"Only once," Leni says. "I thought it was a normal day, but we didn't know it was the last day we'd ever see her. I remember she wore a Minerva pendant around her neck like she wanted us to see. And she *hugged* us before she left for the night. She *never* did that. It wasn't allowed."

Yelena finds herself nodding like that's something that's normal, because of course it isn't. Craving physical affection makes one weak. But the yearning note in Leni's voice when she says the word *hugged* makes something crack in Yelena's chest. She grits her teeth so hard she might crack those, too, but it's better than focusing on whatever this feeling is.

"She never came back," Leni says.

"How long ago was that?"

"I'm not sure. Months ago. The Doctor told us she was on sick leave. But maybe they lied. You said the Doctor lies, so maybe she lied about Miss Irene being sick."

"Maybe," Yelena says, as a farmhouse with paint

peeling in stripes worn smooth by rain comes into view. The tin roof is so rusty it doesn't even try to shine when the sun hits it, and the crumbling fence around the house encircles an overgrown yard.

As Yelena pulls the minivan to a stop, her eyes catch on something peeking out of the tall grass that makes her heart sink. Before she can say anything, Leni unbuckles her seat belt and dashes out of the van.

"Oh no," Yelena says under her breath, scrambling for her own belt and getting out. "Hey!" she calls. "Slow down. We need to make sure the area's secure."

But it's too late to distract her. Leni's spotted it, too.

The farmhouse, like a few that they passed on their trip through the fields of corn, has a family graveyard.

This farmhouse has a fresh grave. Leni falls to her knees in front of it, her face twisting in pain as she reads the words carved into the stone.

IRENE MURPHY
BELOVED SISTER AND SCIENTIST

Below the epitaph is a quote. *"I don't wish to be without my brains, tho' they doubtless interfere with a blind faith which would be very comfortable."*

"Ada Lovelace said that," Leni says. "Miss Irene used to tell Leah about her."

"I'm sorry, Leni," Yelena says, but Leni shakes her head, rejecting any sympathy. When her eyes meet Yelena's, the expression in them . . .

Yelena recognizes it, and she wishes she didn't.

"I've got no one," Leni whispers. "I don't even know if I believe you that you didn't kill Miss Bess."

Yelena's throat clicks on her hard swallow.

"You—"

"You forget," Leni says. "I'm not just your genetic double. I was raised to be wary of the Source."

"Leni—" Yelena hates how much it hurts, to be called that after several days of Leni using her name.

But Leni's on her feet, rushing up the porch steps before Yelena can do anything—stop her, yell at her, secure the farmhouse. She reaches out to snatch her back by the neck of her shirt, but Leni's too fast, fueled by grief and the realization Yelena had around her age: *I'm on my own.*

Yelena chases after her, up the creaking stairs, through the unlocked front door. The foyer is dark, her eyes taking a second to adjust to the dimness as she blinks.

The creak of a floorboard. A whimper. Yelena's eyes fly up.

She freezes.

"Don't move," Johanna says from the top of the stairs.

Her eyes glint with triumph as she begins to take the steps down.

"Because I'm really going to obey you," Yelena says. "I bet you're pleased—you got the jump on me for once."

"Some of us know how to track," Johanna says. "And others don't know how to hide their tracks."

Yelena catches sight of movement over Johanna's shoulder. Leni. She's got the tote bag of books, winding up to swing it down on Johanna's head like a truncheon.

Johanna's halfway down the stairs. Leni just needs to let loose at the right moment.

"There's no use running," Johanna says, mistaking the way Yelena tenses for a fight-or-flight instinct. "You're surrounded."

Yelena gives Leni the slightest of nods. She lets the tote bag fly.

"You have terrible spatial awareness," Yelena says, right before the tote bag full of heavy books collides with the back of Johanna's head.

21.
THE FARMHOUSE

LOCATION: KANSAS
OBJECTIVE: DEFEAT JOHANNA AND TEAM

Unfortunately, the books aren't heavy enough to knock Johanna unconscious. She pitches forward and lands with a practiced twist, her momentum stalled as she grabs the banister.

"Run! Hide!" Yelena barks at Leni, who scrambles down the hall, out of sight.

The profound relief at Leni actually obeying her almost knocks a hole in Yelena's stomach. All she has to do is take down Johanna . . . and whatever team's accompanied her. Then she can grab Leni and run.

Run where? She has no idea. She'll figure it out later. First thing: Deal with Johanna.

"I knew there was something wrong with you as soon as I met you," Johanna says, using the banister to wrench herself to her feet. She takes the steps two at a time, landing with a thump at the bottom, just feet away from Yelena. "But I didn't clock you as being stupid enough to be a traitor. Do you know how angry Director Cady is?"

"I don't care," Yelena says. "I don't serve him. My commander is not your commander, Johanna."

"Well, *my* commander's directed me to bring you and the girl in. That's exactly what we're going to do."

Bring you and the girl in.

Director Cady wants them alive, then. Interesting. It's an advantage Yelena didn't think she'd be handed, considering she ruined an assassination mission when she grabbed Leni instead of killing her. Something has changed Cady's mind. Does he not want to kill Leni now?

Did he never want to? Was it the Doctor's decision? Are they at odds?

Yelena doesn't have time to puzzle out answers to the questions whirring in her mind. There's a snick of a door opening next to her. Her eyes dart to the right. Crystal steps into the hallway, moving steadily, a tranquilizer gun pointed directly at Yelena.

"Put that down before you hurt yourself," Yelena says. "You've got it set on reverse."

Crystal glances down to check the switch and Yelena seizes upon the momentary distraction, lashing out and grasping her wrist, twisting painfully so the tranquilizer gun clatters to the ground. She kicks it away, sending it spinning under a dusty bookcase.

Crystal dives for it—and lands right up against Yelena as a result.

"Crystal!" Johanna hisses angrily, halting at the bottom of the stairs.

"I didn't—" Crystal squeaks as Yelena positions the smaller girl in front of her as a shield. She frisks her, removing a knife and her Widow's Bite bracelets as Johanna watches, waiting for an in.

Yelena's bracelet sparks dangerously close to Crystal's neck. She whimpers, her eyes widening like a horse seeing fire for the first time.

"Where is the rest of your team?" Yelena demands, keeping Crystal in front of her so Johanna can't strike. She got the measure of Johanna early. Severely injuring Crystal to get to Yelena would be a pleasure for Johanna. She wouldn't even blink. But she'd need to strike at the right time.

That's what you have to do, to be the best.

"I told you, Yelena," Johanna says with a smirk. "You're surrounded."

"You're down one girl," Yelena says, her grip tightening on Crystal. "Two, if you count me."

"I don't," Johanna says.

"So that leaves Celia and Tiffany," Yelena says. "What did you do? Station one on the back porch and one on the front?"

Johanna flushes, which tells Yelena she's nailed it. She grins. That means Leni's safe upstairs. "You think

Tiff's using that porch swing? You know how she loves to sprawl over things."

"She wouldn't dare—" Johanna starts to say, and then she shuts herself right up. Giving way too much away.

"Do I sense tension in the ranks?" Yelena leans forward so her cheek almost brushes Crystal's. She trembles at the near touch.

"What do you think, Crys?" Yelena asks. "Is Johanna here doing a good job as team leader? Or was I better?"

"Yelena, you turned traitor! You're a kidnapper!" Crystal practically shrieks.

"But I didn't yell at you when I was leading the team, did I?" Yelena asks, and Crystal frowns.

"Okay, no, you didn't," Crystal admits.

"And Johanna does, doesn't she?"

"That's not the— I mean, yes, but . . . you're confusing me!"

"Don't engage with her," Johanna orders, her eyes widening as she catches on to Yelena's game.

"It's kind of hard not to when she's inches away from shocking me!" Crystal snaps. "Do something!"

Yelena almost giggles. There's *definitely* tension in the ranks. "She's not going to do anything," she tells Crystal. "She doesn't care if you live or die. All she cares about is the mission."

"She needs me for the mission!" Crystal says.

Yelena smirks. "Does she?"

Crystal stiffens in her grip.

"Don't let her get in your head," Johanna says, her eyes widening. "Stay calm. We've got her outnumbered."

"I don't see your other two teammates running to help," Yelena says. "And I've got you, don't I, Crystal?" She sparks her Widow's Bite, close enough to almost singe Crystal's cheek.

"As soon as I yell—" Johanna threatens.

Yelena doesn't hesitate. She presses her bracelet against Crystal's neck, the crackle-snap of the electricity filling the air as Crystal slumps to the ground.

Johanna leaps like she's been waiting, too. Yelena darts back, but it's not far enough. Just like their cage-match fight—was it really only days ago?—their bodies collide in a great crash through the French doors, glass shattering everywhere. The enormous wooden dining table takes up much of the room, and Yelena's eyes dart to the heavy-looking silver candlesticks set on them.

She's dimly aware of shouting in the distance—either Tiffany or Celia, now alerted to the commotion inside the house—but then she's too busy trying to keep Johanna from strangling her to pay attention to much else.

She kicks Johanna in the stomach, but even that doesn't loosen the girl's punishing grip on her neck. Her fingers dig so tight Yelena's vision begins to dance with black spots. Her eyes feel like they're about to pop out of her skull.

"Johanna, you'll kill her!" someone shrieks, and then the weight's lifted off her and Yelena doesn't even have time to cough or suck in air; instead, she rolls. She keeps rolling away from Johanna's lethal hold until she's rolled under the enormous table. From this angle she can see: Celia is the one who pulled Johanna off her. Footsteps in the hall and then boots in the doorway. That'll be Tiffany.

"Gang's all here," Yelena says, her voice hoarse.

"Get the girl! She's somewhere upstairs!" Johanna tells the boots.

"Don't even think about it." Yelena pushes herself out from under the table, grabbing the candlestick holder. She barely has time to make sure it's heavy enough in her hand before she hurls it straight at a startled Tiffany's head.

Tiffany ducks at the last moment, but it's enough of a distraction. Yelena charges at her, snapping out her leg with precision born of constant practice. Tiffany never had a chance. She lands hard on the ground.

"Get her!" Yelena hears Johanna scream, but she's already running, stepping over Tiffany before she dashes into the hall and up the stairs and then she's screaming too, louder even than Johanna. But she's screaming Leni's name.

A flicker of movement out of the corner of her eye. She has a split second to react. There's an old mirror set on the wall and she grabs it, flinging it like an oversize Frisbee down the stairs. Johanna's scream cuts off—so surprised and abrupt that Yelena thinks for a moment that she's decapitated her or something. But then the enraged yell tells her no, she's not that lucky.

"Leni!" she yells, jerking open the first door she sees. The room's empty. She hurries to the next one.

"Yelena!"

There she is. Peeking out from underneath a dusty chenille blanket that hangs over a brass bed. Yelena slams the bedroom door shut behind her, looking around—not frantically, never frantically. She will remain calm. She will remain clearheaded.

Leni needs her to be.

There's a wooden dresser on the other side of the door. Heavy-looking oak. She pushes it across the floor, blocking the door, before dashing over to the bed.

Yelena grabs Leni's arm, dragging her out when she hears footsteps over broken glass as the team slowly begins to make their way over the shattered mirror and up the stairs.

Good. They've learned to be cautious. They've learned

they have to be when it comes to her. That gives her time, and that's what she needs.

"We're going to put these on you," Yelena says, snapping open the bracelets she took off Crystal and putting them on Leni's wrists. "I'll teach you to use them properly later. Just press here if anyone gets too close, okay?" She taps the small manual button at the bottom. Leni nods as Yelena programs the bracelets to *stun* with a simple touch. It's a cold move, but she sets the stun to double the power . . . just to make sure anyone who gets knocked out *stays* knocked out. Whoever receives the shock will live, but they'll have a killer headache for a good week after they wake up.

"This way. Hurry," she says, taking Leni over to the window and pushing it up with a creak. She looks down and sees the porch roof is below. Perfect. Her chest tightens at how far the drop is. One of them might break a bone or two. But it's better than trying to go through the rest of the team to get downstairs. That way ends in death, maybe even theirs. This way, well, maybe still ends in death, but maybe *not* theirs.

The bedroom doorknob rattles and loosens as the door knocks against the dresser, unable to swing open.

"She's barricaded the door," Johanna yells. "Get an ax or something!"

"Up." Yelena boosts Leni into the window, her legs

dangling in the open air. Leni's shoulders tense under her hands as her eyes settle on the porch roof.

"That's really far."

"Tuck your arms like this." Yelena folds her arms across her chest. If she uses them to brace her fall, she'll break her wrists. "I want you to push *gently* off the sill. When you hit the roof, I want you to *roll*. Roll like a wheel, straight down."

Leni swallows. "Okay," she says, sounding so unsure that Yelena changes her mind in a flash.

"Never mind. Scoot," she says, nudging Leni with her hip. She obeys and Yelena squeezes in next to her. It's a tight fit, even as she wraps her arms around Leni. *It's not a hug*, she tells herself.

"On three," she says. "One. Two. *Three*."

She pushes off the windowsill, twisting in the air as they fall so that she's cradling Leni protectively, her shoulders taking the entire jolting force of the fall. The breath's knocked out of her, the pain in her lungs as she fights for air too sharp as the pressure of Leni's weight adds to the struggle.

"Off," she chokes out, pushing gently. Leni scrambles to her feet. "Go," Yelena manages to spit out between coughs, pointing to the drainpipe. Above them, she hears the shattering of wood, and she doesn't have time to shimmy down the drainpipe like Leni—she just pitches herself off the porch roof. Tranquilizer darts embed themselves in a neat line along the roof just inches away from where she just landed.

She's still trying to catch her breath, so she just points toward the cornfield. Leni gets her meaning and runs into the cover of the tall stalks. The rows of corn are tall, since they aren't ready to be harvested yet, providing great cover for running through the gaps between the plants.

"Keep quiet and move fast," Yelena whispers as she hears shouting in the distance, growing nearer with every second that ticks by. They pass under a scarecrow, set on a tall enough pole to overlook the crop.

Yelena holds out her fist to indicate Leni should stop, but the little girl just shoots her a puzzled look. Right. She isn't the clone who was taught military tactics or strategy or how to fight. That would be Ellie.

Stop, she mouths at Leni.

They crouch under the scarecrow as Yelena does a quick circle, trying to decide the best direction. Going straight would take them farther into the crop; taking a right might lead them to a more open field or endless cornstalks. A left would put them on the road . . . if Johanna doesn't catch them first.

Staying under the cover of the crop is the best move, Yelena decides. She bends, digging in her pocket. Without the tote bag, lost back at the house after Leni threw it at Johanna, they're down to what's in her pockets. So that means they've got four sticks of acid gum, their bracelets, and that's about it. She had left Crystal's knife in the glove compartment of the car because Leni kept messing with it while they drove. That girl and dangerous things!

She peels a small sliver of the gum off one piece, sticking it to the bottom of the scarecrow's post. It slowly begins to eat away at the wood.

"Let's move," Yelena says. Johanna will regroup and come after them at any moment. Hopefully the scarecrow falling will prove a distraction—momentary or otherwise.

Cornstalks whip across her face, scratchy and annoying, but she ducks her head and focuses on shielding Leni. With every step, she's afraid she'll feel the shock of electricity from someone's bracelet or the sting of a tranquilizer dart, but there's nothing.

Crack! The sound of wood breaking echoes dully behind them. The scarecrow's gone down, the acid gum fully eating away at the post. The commotion is quickly followed by shouting and then rustling.

Her suspicions were confirmed. They're not alone in the field.

"Keep moving!" Yelena urges, but as she glances over her shoulder down the row, she can see a glimpse of Johanna heading straight toward them.

"Belova!" Johanna shouts.

Yelena slides her arm under Leni's, picking her up, then runs down the rows of corn as fast as she can.

"Yelena, I can't!" Leni protests as Yelena half carries, half drags her through the cornfield, frantically searching for a place to hide. But Yelena can see it ahead: where the cornfield stops and opens up.

They're stuck. Johanna has driven them straight out into the open. No cover. Nowhere to hide. But there's no choice. Johanna's too close behind.

At least she's got her orders to take us alive, Yelena thinks, her hands tightening around Leni as the corn stalks brush against her face like trailing fingers.

"Belova!" Johanna bellows behind them again and Yelena picks up speed, Leni clutched tight against her as they burst out of the shadow of the cornfield and into the light.

For a moment, all she sees is the fence, and she dashes toward it, the only thought to get them both over it.

And that's when she sees the sign.

WORLD'S BIGGEST BALL OF TWINE

An incredulous smile spreads across her face as she realizes the empty field she thought they were headed toward is actually a field turned parking lot, graveled over for tourists, with a half dozen cars and at least one school bus parked. There's a group of children led by what looks like a very stressed teacher walking down the path toward the attraction.

"Get yourself lost in that crowd of kids," she urges Leni, pushing her forward. The teacher is so harried, she won't notice an extra head. Thankfully, Leni doesn't even look back to see if Yelena's following her; she just obeys, disappearing into the crowd as they head toward the attraction.

Yelena hears the cornstalks rustle behind her, and her body hums with a dreadful anticipation as she springs into action. Just as Johanna breaks through the cornfield at full tilt, she runs right into Yelena's outstretched arm, forcing her back into the depth of the crop, away from the parking lot, and out of sight of the retreating Leni.

Johanna lets out a pained grunt as Yelena's strength drives her off-balance. It's a classic move. But it's a move that works a bit differently when one is short. A taller person would've been able to catch Johanna at the chest, perhaps breaking a rib or two before she was forced to the ground.

Unfortunately, Yelena's always been lacking in the height department—which does make fitting into small spaces convenient, and fortunately, it means that Yelena's arm hits Johanna straight in the gut, not the chest. Those squishy places are unprotected by bones. Vulnerable and soft.

Yelena would almost feel sorry for Johanna's surely soon-to-be-bleeding spleen, but she's too busy placing her boot on Johanna's throat.

"Traitor," Johanna spits.

"You need new material," Yelena says. "But I understand: It's been a stressful few days. Where are the others?"

Johanna laughs. There's blood on her lips. She must've bitten her cheek as she went down.

Amateur.

"Where do you think? I sent them ahead."

Yelena's eyes widen as Johanna's laughter rises to an unhinged level. "I don't know why you're so obsessed with the girl. But she's not getting away this time. And neither are you."

Yelena doesn't even bother to use her Widow's Bite. She just pulls her foot off Johanna's neck and swings it back. When her boot collides with Johanna's face, she doesn't lie to herself.

She's holding back nothing.

22.
THE WORLD'S BIGGEST BALL OF TWINE

LOCATION: KANSAS
OBJECTIVE: EVASION

*F*ind Leni.

Yelena races across the gravel parking lot and toward the path the class of children had disappeared down. How could she have been so stupid? She should never have let her out of her sight. If Tiffany has her . . . or even worse, if *Crystal* tries something . . .

She'll use the Widow's Bite, like Yelena told her, won't she? Yelena is a little worried that, when it comes down to it, Leni won't want to hurt anyone . . . even if her own life is at stake.

The Doctor let Leni's handler nurture her heart and soul, whatever those things really mean. Yelena thought she was devoid of them, but the proof . . .

The proof is right in front of her. *You could be this. You could be anything. That's what it is to be formed by someone instead of loved by them.*

All of them—Yelena, Leni, her sisters—they are nothing but clay to be molded.

She knew that, somehow. She just didn't care, before.

And now she is stuck in an *after* she cannot free herself from.

Yelena turns the corner on the path, the ground sloping downward slightly as the crowd of people milling around the giant ball of twine comes into sight. Using the vantage point, Yelena frantically scans the group, looking for blond hair. That crooked braid she had woven into Leni's hair last night herself.

She can't spot the braid—or Leni—anywhere. Did Tiffany grab her already? Toss her in a van with Celia driving and disappear in a cloud of dust?

Her chest tightens, and for a moment she clutches it, the pain so sharp she's sure she's been shot or stabbed. She's sure if she turns, she'll see Johanna standing there, a knife in hand.

But no, this pain is just from the thought of losing Leni. What has Yelena become?

Like Leni. She's become like Leni. All heart when she's supposed to be heartless.

It's the height of irony. Leni and her sisters were raised to be even better than Yelena. And just days spent in the little clone's presence and Yelena has gone all gooey like Leni instead.

She should've seen it coming. She'd told the girl herself that if you can read people, you can manipulate them.

And here she is, stripped of her training, of her cruelty, of her callousness, of her focus and mission, on the edge of a panic attack at the thought of losing the girl she promised to protect.

It was a lie, you know it was, it doesn't matter what you told her.

But it does.

Her eyes land on an older girl with a baseball cap pulled tightly over her head—over her *undercut*.

Tiffany. Yelena's moving before she fully thinks out a plan. She races toward the shingled pavilion housing the giant ball of twine that hangs from a thick chain, hovering above the ground. She loses sight of Tiffany's ball cap in the crowd, getting caught behind a family taking picture after picture of the ball of twine like they need to capture it from all angles.

Where is she? Yelena pushes past the family, her worry mounting. She has to get to Leni before Tiffany does. . . .

A hand clamps down on her bicep. She jerks instinctively away from it, whirling, fists raising. But when her eyes meet the same blue as hers, it almost knocks her off her feet, the relief.

"I saw the curly-haired one," Leni says.

"That's Celia," Yelena says. "She and Tiffany are here. We need a distraction so we can get to the parking lot and steal another car."

She needs to lift someone's car keys from their purse.

Yelena wishes she had some sort of explosive, but all she has left are three and a half sticks of acid gum.

"There!" Leni points across the way. On the other side of the giant ball of twine stand Celia and Tiffany, their heads bent as they talk together.

"Don't point." Yelena snatches her hand down, resisting the urge to grab her and flatten them both to the ground. Her mind flies through the possibilities—the number of people who could be harmed, the mess that will descend if one of the girls starts shooting electroshocks or tranquilizer darts into a crowd of children.

"Gimme the gum," Leni says suddenly. "I have an idea."

"What?" Yelena asks, but before she can stop her, Leni snatches almost all the gum out of her pocket and darts over to the pulley that's keeping the ball of twine suspended.

"Oh, you really are me," she mutters as Leni smashes the last pieces of acid gum together and slams the entire wad against the pulley before backing away. Yelena zeroes in on her task: finding someone's keys to steal. The mom corralling the three kids in front of her is so harried that she hasn't noticed that her purse isn't zipped up. Easy pickings. She's got the keys in her hands in less than twenty seconds. Which is about how much time it takes for the acid to eat through the metal and rope of the pulley.

The pulley snaps, the rope and chain holding the suspended twine ball pooling free of the lever, the ball falling to the ground with a heart-shaking thump as people let out startled shrieks. The ground rumbles and vibrates under their feet while the twine ball begins to roll right into the path of Tiffany and Celia.

Celia dives out of the way, but Tiffany disappears out of sight, the ball of twine careening through the crowd.

People scream and scatter as the twine ball begins its path of destruction, building speed with each bounce as it smashes through the pavilion housing it, causing one of the columns to crash down so the entire roof comes sliding off. The twine ball breaks free and coasts downhill as people stumble and fall and others chase after it.

Leni stares, stunned, watching the twine ball like she can't quite believe it worked.

"Good job! Now run!" Yelena says, yanking at her again, thinking she's going to have to teach her better reaction time. This is not the time to gape. This is the time to run.

The chaos of the crowd is perfect to lose themselves in. The parking lot gravel crunches under her feet as she aims the key fob toward the row of cars and one on the end comes to life, the horn beeping cheerily.

"The blue one!" she yells.

But just as they head toward it, a hand slams down on the hood. A half-sagging Johanna stumbles into view, her face masked in bruises and blood.

"BELOVA!" Johanna's pressed against the car like she's not sure she can stand up on her own. Behind them, the giant ball of twine is still causing chaos, rolling through the crowd and toward the cornfield.

Yelena swears under her breath, but not quietly enough, because Leni makes a curious noise.

"Do not repeat that!" she says quickly, realizing that Leni might not know what curse words are. The last thing she needs is for Leni to teach her sisters fun new words when they're reunited.

The easy route out is cut off, and if they head into the chaos that Leni created with the twine ball, they'll run into Tiffany and Celia.

"Keep going toward the barn to my right," she says to Leni softly as she inches slowly toward the car Johanna's using as her support system. She keeps her body angled, blocking Leni from Johanna's line of sight as they slowly walk, step by step, toward the road that leads to the barn down the way.

"Give up now," Johanna pants. "I'll bring you in gently." Blood pours from her nose, but she doesn't seem to notice or care. Johanna's locked in on one thing:

bringing Yelena down. She'd admire the focus, but it's messing up her escape plan and will get them all killed if she's not fast enough.

"You and I know there's nothing gentle about either of us."

Yelena chucks the keys in her hands toward Johanna's injured face with the windup of an all-American pitcher, zapping them in midair with her bracelet so the metal will carry the electric current.

She doesn't even wait to see if they hit her target—she just grabs Leni's hand and then they're running again. It feels like all she's done for days is run, and she wants to stop, but she can't.

She's in too deep, she's gone too far, dived in hand in hand with her mini me, and there's no way out but through.

Just keep moving, she tells herself as Johanna cries out and the smell of singed flesh tells her that her makeshift weapon most certainly hit its target.

She tells herself it doesn't matter. That it doesn't hurt.

But she fears it's not true.

That the real truth lies deeper inside.

That Leni's empathy is something she's capable of, too.

23.
THE BARN

LOCATION: KANSAS
OBJECTIVE: SURVIVE AND FLEE

They kick up dust clouds as they run down the dirt road toward the barn, the sounds of the crowd fading as Yelena bursts through the barn doors, pushing Leni inside and slamming them shut. She barely has time to take a breath before she turns, looking around. She was hoping for a tractor or an old truck or even a horse to work with. But what she sees . . .

"Do you think we can fly that out of here?" Leni asks, pointing to the rickety plane with an open-air cockpit that's taking up most of the barn. A crop duster. Yelena read about them during her briefing on American farmland culture.

"Maybe," Yelena says. "But I don't know where we're going."

"I think I do," Leni says. "I found this in Miss Irene's room, under the bed." She pulls out a folded piece of paper. On it is a sketch of an old neon motel sign for the Sleepy Hollow Motel, a doodle of a cactus, and another drawing—one of what looks like the doors to a bunker set in a sand dune, with coordinates scribbled above it.

"Leni, what's this?" Yelena asks, tapping the sketch.

"That's home," Leni says.

"Do you recognize this motel sign?"

"I'm not sure. I was kind of overwhelmed when Miss Bess brought me through town. I'd never been before. And we drove fast."

The coordinates are something. Coordinates and a plane are more than she had five minutes ago.

"We need to find the keys to the plane." She climbs up into the cockpit to see if they're anywhere inside, but there's nothing. "Leni, help me look," she says when she glances up to see Leni glued to one of the barn windows.

"They're coming," Leni says.

"Get away from the window!" Yelena yells, launching herself out of the cockpit and toward Leni just as the glass shatters.

She tackles her to the ground as something whizzes over their heads, striking the metal hull of the plane with a ping.

"Crawl on your belly!" Yelena says, demonstrating as she moves forward, her stomach grinding into the ground. No more gunfire above their head, which is a relief. But she knows with silence comes strategy. Johanna is out there, and she's planning something.

She's been tasked with bringing them in alive. That means she can't just shoot up the barn. The team has to come in here to grab them. Yelena can use that to her advantage. She just needs to keep Leni out of reach.

"Leni, come here." She rises to a crouch at the bottom of the barn stairs. "I want you to climb up these and get up on that beam." She points to the thick wooden beam that splits the barn, supporting the hayloft. "You need to pick your moment, okay? I can't tell you when. You'll have to listen to your gut. But . . . remember those drop bears you read about?"

Leni's eyes light up with understanding. "Yeah!"

"Take inspiration from that," Yelena says. "Go!"

Leni doesn't hesitate; she scrambles up the stairs and shinnies across the beam. Yelena's heart clenches at the sight of Leni tiptoeing across it like she's doing a gymnastics act. Yelena only breathes easy when Leni takes her place right at the center of it. It positions her perfectly above the plane . . . and whoever approaches it.

Yelena only has a second to scan the area. Luckily, she spots a toolbox. There's no hammer, but there is a screwdriver. It'll have to do. She grabs it and ducks under the plane, lying in wait, clutching her makeshift weapon to her chest, praying Leni will stay out of sight. That she'll pick the right moment.

What if she gets hurt? What if she tries to jump on Johanna and misses?

She breathes deep. She has to trust Leni can do it.

It smells like dust and machine oil under the plane and the tang of it sticks to the back of her throat even when she breathes through her mouth. She tilts her head to get a better look at the door, but instead she notices there's a square of duct tape slapped under the plane. With concentration, she picks at an edge, peeling it away.

A pair of keys falls onto her stomach. She grins. The first bit of luck she's had in a while, and she'll take it.

The barn door rattles as it opens and the shaft of light temporarily obscures her vision until the outline of a ponytail comes into view.

Crystal. It makes sense to Yelena: send in the weakest link, an operative you can risk losing while the rest of the team covers all other possible exits.

She breathes quietly, waiting for Crystal's feet to come into sight. Her hand closes around the screwdriver. One more step, and . . .

Crystal stops. Yelena's sure she's been made. Her fingers tightens around the shiv. It's now or never.

She rolls free of her hiding place. Crystal lets out a startled yelp that morphs into a scream when Yelena punches the screwdriver into her calf and then yanks it out. Blood blossoms as Crystal falls back with a whimper, clutching at her leg.

Yelena doesn't hesitate. The charge of the Widow's Bite laces through Crystal, her body jerking to the electro-shock before her eyes flutter shut.

She barely has the time to drag Crystal's body under the plane and roll back under it herself before she hears the rattle of the door again. Johanna is sending her team in one by one to be picked off. Why? There's safety in numbers and brute force.

Yelena's missing something, but she doesn't know what it is. It sends an unsettling charge of nervous energy through her that has nothing to do with electricity.

She tilts her head out from under the plane enough to confirm Leni is still crouched on the beam, tucked up high and safe . . . for now.

"Yelena?"

It isn't Leni.

It's *Celia*. Calling her name like she's expecting Yelena to answer.

"Yelena, I know you're in here," Celia says. Yelena watches her feet move past the plane, but she doesn't move to cut her like she did Crystal. Something holds her back. She tells herself it's strategy, not friendship. "I know you're scared," Celia continues. "You've made mistakes. But if you just come quietly, it'll look a lot better. If you just stop fighting us, maybe it won't be as bad.

I can't make any promises, but I can try to make your case. But you've got to stop this right now. You've got to give the package up and come with us."

It's a full-body skin-crawl, her reaction to the words *the package*. Because she's not that. She's a person. She's *Leni*. And Yelena knows it shouldn't matter. Her training tells her it doesn't. Only the mission does.

But her brain's been revolting since she saw Leni and her body's been following and her hand is clenching around that shiv again because she doesn't want to stab Celia, but she will if she has to and this entire experience has taught her she has to do a lot of things she doesn't want to do.

"I really think Director Cady's changed his mind," Celia continues. "I don't think he wants to kill the package. So really, there's no reason not to give her up."

Yelena almost snorts. Does Celia believe such obvious lies?

Celia's feet are almost out of sight. Yelena needs to move now. Her arms tense. Her hips shift as she tracks Celia's feet.

But Celia steps to the right instead of the left, almost as if she's spotted something.

Like she's spotted *Leni*.

"AHHHHHHH!" There's an ungodly shriek, high-pitched and nervous, but the leap that Leni makes off the beam is anything but nervous. She swan-dives off, and for a second it seems like she floats, her arc downward almost graceful before she full-body *slams* into a yelping Celia.

Celia flies backward at the force of the blow and momentum, dust spraying everywhere as they tumble to the ground. Leni holds her stolen bracelet against Celia's neck. "Don't make me do it," she says to the older girl.

Yelena scrambles out from under her hiding place. "Sorry, Celia," she says, knocking her out with a quick jabbing shock to the back of the neck.

Leni looks up at Yelena, her eyes wide, her lip trembling.

"Don't you dare start crying," Yelena orders. "There's still two more we've got to deal with."

"Is she dead?" Leni asks.

"I just knocked her out!" Yelena says. "She's my friend, you know."

"You're not very nice to your friends."

"Only because all my friends are trying to kidnap *you*," Yelena says. "Come on, I found the plane keys."

Yelena moves the unconscious Crystal and Celia out of the way of the path of the plane as Leni climbs into the cockpit. Peeking through the broken barn window carefully, Yelena spots Johanna leaning lopsidedly against the fence outside, staring at the barn like it's a puzzle she needs to crack. Tiffany's nowhere in sight. Did the ball of twine take her down? Or is that just Yelena's wishful thinking?

She moves in a low crouch over to the plane, pulling the blocks from under the wheels free before climbing up into the cockpit.

"Ready?" she asks Leni.

"Not even a little," Leni says. "But we have to, right?"

"I'm pretty sure it's the only way," Yelena says, thinking of Johanna waiting outside. Even if she is the only one left and Tiffany was injured by the twine ball, she'll have already called in reinforcements. They'll be arriving any moment.

Yelena's fingers curl over the controllers as she scans the dashboard, trying to summon every memory of every flight simulator she's ever trained on. The engine sputters to life at the turn of the key, the propeller starting slowly and then spinning faster and faster as Yelena swallows hard and pushes on the throttle.

"Keep your head down!" she yells over the roar of the engine as they begin to turn toward the barn door they're going to have to smash through. Yelena bites the inside of her lip and steels her nerve as she pushes down on the throttle. The plane leaps forward, the sudden speed smashing the nose of the plane and then the rest through the barn door like a slow-motion bullet. Wood splinters everywhere, barn boards crashing over Yelena's head as the plane gains speed and momentum, plowing through the fence next, through the open field and then rows of corn as Yelena pushes up on the controllers, slow and steady, and she feels the moment the wheels lift free of the ground. Leni lets out a delighted whoop behind her as they climb high and higher in the air, and Yelena keeps telling herself, *Steady, steady, don't freak out, don't let her see how scared you are.*

They soar over the cornfields, leaving Johanna and the defeated team of Widows behind. Yelena knows she should feel relieved, and she does. She knows she should feel triumphant—they won, after all.

But she knows what kind of punishment is waiting her fellow trainees for failing so terribly, and all she can think as they fly away is: *Run as fast as you can.*

24.
IN THE AIR

LOCATION: UNITED STATES
OBJECTIVE: FLY TO HOME BASE

The problem with fleeing in a stolen crop plane under a looming threat is that sometimes you don't have time to check that you have enough fuel. As the hours in the air tick by and Yelena swallows more than a few bugs while following the coordinates on the GPS, she keeps one eye on the gas gauge, her breath quickening with every minute that passes. The arrow keeps creeping toward the *E*, and according to her calculations, they'll run out of gas several miles from where the Doctor's keeping Yelena's other clones.

She's telling herself it'll be fine. That she'll time it correctly as they soar above a small town that isn't much more than a main street and a few side streets set in the desert. But as they pass over civilization and head farther and farther across the sand, the lights of the town fade and it gets darker. Yelena's eyes zip back and forth between the ground below and the dashboard. She can see sand dunes ahead, a large formation of them, looming high on the ground. Does she have enough fuel to make it?

"Hold on," she shouts, hoping Leni can hear her. "We're going to start our descent."

As she shifts the controllers, tilting the nose down, she's aiming for a slow and steady dip, but her timing is off—she doesn't quite have the feel for it. The nose dips too low, too fast, and when she tries to tilt back up to compensate and even them out, the old engine hiccups in protest at the sudden change with so little fuel.

For a moment, she thinks it's going to be all right. And then the engine goes from hiccupping to full-on sputtering, gasping on what little fuel is left until it dies completely.

In that horrible second of sudden silence, she can hear Leni suck in a breath, too startled to even scream, and then Yelena's not listening anymore; her entire focus is on trying to get the plane to coast on the air as they go down, the ground getting closer and closer with each beat of Yelena's heart.

"Brace!" Yelena screams as they glide right onto the top of a sand dune, skimming across the sand like a rock skipping across a pond, each screeching spray of sand and metal rattling her teeth until they finally skid to a stop.

Smoke fills the air—the engine is maybe on fire—and she blinks dazedly at the curling black pouring out of the nose of the plane, trying to remember why that's bad.

The metal surrounding her is starting to get hot. She squirms in her seat.

Oh, right, fire burns. She needs to get out of the plane.

Yelena coughs out sand—a lot of it—and then lets out an incredulous whoop. "I was a little scared there for a second," she admits. "You okay back there, kid?"

There's no answer. It takes a moment for Yelena's adrenaline to simmer down enough to realize her heart's beating fast for an entirely different reason.

"Leni?" Yelena asks, peering behind her. A free fall inside her stomach when she sees Leni and realizes there's blood trickling down her forehead. "Leni!"

She tears out of the cockpit and into the copilot's seat, lifting Leni out by hooking her hands under her arms and dragging her limp body out. "No, no," Yelena says, her hands pressing against the inside of Leni's wrist. She can't find it. *She can't find it.*

Her hands fly to the girl's neck instead, pressing under her ear, and she lets out a sob of relief when she feels the pulse, weak but there.

Yelena checks Leni's head. She's only bleeding from a cut on her forehead—it looks like she slammed her head against the windshield, if the cracked glass is any indication.

She's stunned. Just knocked out. She's not really hurt. It's okay. She's fine. She'll wake up any second. It's just a bump on the head. She'll be fine. She'll wake up. She'll be fine. It's fine. She's fine.

For a long time, Yelena isn't aware that she's speaking the words out loud.

For even longer, she doesn't realize that the grubby wetness gathering against her cheeks is a combination of tears, blood, and sand.

But when she does, there is no running away from it any longer.

There is just the little girl in her arms—a version of her that she never got to be—and the truth.

That giving her up to the Red Room would be like giving up a piece of herself.

25.
HOME BASE

LOCATION: ARIZONA
OBJECTIVE: BETRAYAL

The ten minutes that Leni is unconscious feel like ten years. Yelena gives up trying to wake her after a minute and instead settles into a quiet waiting that builds something brick by brick inside her. Every second weighs her down further, until she's sure that she'll sink into the sand like it's turned to quicksand.

She regrets ever taking this mission to America. She was so proud when the Commander chose her. Cocky that out of everyone, she had been selected. That he trusted her.

She betrayed him. Took that trust and tore it in half. She should've contacted the Commander days ago. But she didn't. She told herself she would get to this point, where she is right now, and she'd make the right choice. The safe one.

She would do anything to save herself.

Now all she can think about is saving Leni.

Would she feel this way about any child whose path crossed hers like Leni's did?

She wants to say yes, but she's not sure that's the truth. She thinks, perhaps, this was a perfect storm of circumstance. Meeting a more-than-a-twin. Something greater than a sister.

A scientific homage to the strength of her abilities as a spy. Isn't that what Leni and her sisters are? Isn't that why Yelena was chosen?

Next to her, Leni stirs. Yelena's hand cups her cheek gently as the girl's eyes slowly flutter open, hazy at first in the dim moonlight. "Careful," Yelena says as Leni tries to sit up. "You knocked your head pretty hard."

"I'm fine," Leni says, but it takes her two tries to get to her feet and even then, she sways a little. "I saw these dunes when Miss Bess took me. We're on the wrong side of them."

"Are the bunker doors on the other side?"

Leni nods. "A few miles that way." She points. "But we don't need to go that far. We're going to go in the way Miss Bess took me out. There's an emergency tunnel that lets out into this trapdoor north of the facility's main doors."

"Is it guarded?"

"It wasn't when we escaped," Leni says.

"That might have changed," Yelena says. "Does it open from the outside *and* the inside?"

Leni nods. "Miss Bess made me memorize the override code. Just in case we got separated in the desert."

"What's the code?"

"Two six seven nine," Leni says.

"Okay, are you good to go?" Yelena asks. "Make sure to use those bracelets if you need to, do you hear me?"

Leni nods. "I will," she says. "To protect my sisters."

Yelena's stomach twists at the thought of the other two, somewhere under the sand right now, tucked in their little bunker world, not knowing their sister is coming for them.

Or maybe they do. Maybe they believe in her and in each other the way that Leni seems to believe in them.

I didn't know about sisters. Leni's confession rings in her ears.

Some things you know, even if you don't have words for it. This is what Leni is teaching her. And some things you learn, even if you don't want to.

Trudging through the sand is a struggle. Yelena's thighs burn as they walk, her pace slower than she'd like because of Leni's much shorter legs. The girl doesn't complain, Yelena will give her that. But her lips get more and more pinched the farther they walk, her eyes fixed on the horizon like she's looking for a landmark.

It strikes Yelena in that moment, with sand whipping at her cheeks and lips, her throat parched and dying for a sip of water, that she's put a considerable amount of trust into her clone. For all she knows, Leni could be leading her to her death.

Yet she just continues to follow her.

"We'll be there in a little bit," Leni says, but the more minutes tick by, the slower she gets. Moving through the sand seems to be a fight.

"Do you need to rest?" Yelena asks.

"I need to get to my sisters," Leni insists. "We're close. I know it."

Yelena hesitates. Her body feels heavy. She has to do this and take the opening. If she lets Leni take her through the back way, she can lead her right into Director Cady's hands. She can trade her back for safe passage home. Director Cady won't kill her, that much she knows. Even if he has informed the Red Room of her so-called betrayal, the Commander will want to deal with her himself. That means she needs to be taken in alive.

Commander Starkovsky will understand once she explains what the Outpost is up to without his permission.

She just needs to let Leni show her the back door and lead the girl into a trap. A simple, efficient solving of the problem.

But Yelena can't see Leni that way any longer. Yelena's feet won't move. Her mind can't see Leni as a tool or a trade or a target anymore.

What has become of her? She may never know. She may always have to hide from this part of herself after this moment. But in this moment . . .

In this moment, she wants to be good.

"Leni, wait a second," she says. She sounds tinny to her own ears, and Leni must hear it, too, because she frowns. She reaches out and stills Yelena's suddenly shaking hand before pulling away.

"I want you to listen to me," Yelena says, kneeling in the sand so that they're at eye level. "You need to understand: If we go in that bunker, you're never coming out."

Leni's eyes are so clear when they meet Yelena's. There's no shock in her face, and no fear, either. Instead, there is pity as her hands cup Yelena's face gently.

"Because you're going to trade me so you're not in trouble anymore," Leni says.

"Yes," Yelena says.

A smile stretches her bruised face. "No," she says simply.

". . . No?" Yelena echoes.

"No," Leni says. "You're not going to do that. If you were, you wouldn't give me an out right now. You're trying to make me run and leave my sisters behind."

Yelena licks her lips, hating how neatly she's been trapped. She might as well leap into the fray.

"You're free right now. If you go right now, if you run, I can let you." She hates the pleading in her voice. "I won't chase after you. I give you my word. But if we go inside..."

"You'll have to turn me over?"

Yelena won't say it. That she's scared of being faced with the choice. She was acting on sheer shock and instinct in the penthouse when she first saw Leni. But she's adjusted. She's had time to think and time for the shock to fade. She's been left with the terrible consequences of the last week as they fled and tried to survive and figure out what to do.

A part of her yearns for the safety and routine of home. Of knowing herself and her purpose with no question. Most of her hates that she's here, that Leni has infected her, shifting how she sees things and herself so monumentally she's still reeling.

But some of her doesn't hate Leni at all. Something lurks in that organ in her chest that she's long thought of as a muscle and nothing more.

"You can be selfish," Yelena says. "I know you can be."

"And *you* can be selfless," Leni shoots back. "You're just choosing not to be."

The disappointment in her little face is like a stinging blow. And then Yelena realizes with a sick slide into shock that comes too late... that the stinging... it's *real*. She's been stabbed with something sharp right under her ear.

The little brat's injected her with the paralytic! She's clutching the tube of lipstick in her hand. She must've stolen it and kept it tucked in her pocket this whole time.

Leni steps away as Yelena falls backward, her entire body stiff and unmoving, her eyes wide and fixed on the night sky. She's unable to latch onto anything to steady her panic until Leni pops into view, staring down at her.

"Sorry," Leni says. "But you were right: I'm good at reading people. And manipulating them. When I almost ate the gum and realized all your stuff was dangerous, I stole your lipstick out of the hands-off tote bag. I saw it had an injector, I figured it'd take you down once you got me back home. I hoped I wouldn't have to use it. But I was prepared to do what I had to. I'm *not* leaving without my sisters."

"Leni," Yelena tries to say, but her tongue is not cooperating, so it just comes out as a garbled sound. If she goes in there alone . . .

Oh god, what did she do by trying to warn her? She was so stupid to assume Leni would be selfish like her.

"You'll be safe here," Leni says, like she's trying to convince herself. "The guards don't come out this far on their night patrols. When the paralytic wears off . . . well, it's your choice, I guess. You have the back-door code.

You could come help me. Or you can wait for us to come back. Or you can leave. I won't blame you if you leave, Yelena. Really, I won't. But I want you to know . . ." Leni swallows, her throat bobbing nervously as she searches for the words. "It's okay to be hurt by what they did to you. And it's okay to admit they hurt you. They hurt me. But they didn't break me."

A tear leaks out of the corner of Yelena's eye. It's the strangest muted feeling. She can barely feel it, but the ghost of moisture makes her wonder if the paralytic is wearing off even quicker than Leni expected.

If she can stop her . . . if she can drag her away from this . . .

"Thank you for getting me here," Leni says. "I have to go now."

She steps out of view.

No! Yelena desperately tries to move. To turn her head, to track Leni's movement. She has to get up. But the paralytic coursing through her system is too much. She can't fight through it yet.

She strains her ears for sounds, for any indication that Leni is still nearby, but there's nothing.

Yelena lies there, frozen in the sand, as Leni gets farther and farther out of reach.

26.
HOME BASE

LOCATION: ARIZONA
OBJECTIVE: FREEDOM

The flicker of the lights in the playroom is the first thing that tells Leah something is wrong. They only flicker like that when the backup generator kicks in.

She doesn't look up from the card game she and Ellie are playing. But she taps out a message on her knee: *Someone's here.*

It's the opening they've been waiting for. The backup generator only activates when the bunker's main or back doors are open. It'll take several minutes for the cameras to reboot in the process.

Ellie gives her the barest nod. "Do you have any sevens?"

"Go fish," Leah tells her, tilting her cards down just enough for Ellie to see that she's got three sevens, actually.

It's their agreed-upon signal. Ellie reaches over to the bag of baby carrots they've been sharing, taking a too-big handful and stuffing them in her mouth. She chews poorly and then swallows dramatically, sputtering as she pretends to choke on the vegetables.

Even Leah's impressed with how real it looks. Ellie goes *bright* red as they both get to their feet.

"Oh my gosh!" Leah yelps. She frantically runs to the door, pounding on it. "Help! Help! She's choking!"

Ellie staggers behind her, pretending to be dazed from the rapid oxygen loss, but really she's heading toward the pile of toys where they've tucked Leah's special smoke solution.

"Help!" Leah yells again, jumping back from the door as she hears footsteps rushing down the hall.

The door swings open. Ellie's fingers close over the bottle full of purple liquid as Leah faces the security guard who stands at the ready in the doorway, but he does not cross into the room. The Doctor has strict rules about who is allowed inside their playroom. Scientists only.

"What's going on?" he asks harshly.

"We need help!" Leah says, flinging her arm behind her to indicate a rapidly purpling Ellie.

"Oh boy," the guy says. He pulls out his radio, flipping it on with a click. "We're going to need a med—"

An electric zip sizzles through the air and the security guard lets out a strange, full-body jerk before he starts to fall forward. Leah scrambles out of the way with a frightened "Eep!" as the man smashes face-first into the concrete floor, revealing the person standing behind him.

"Leni!" Leah hurls herself at her sister, wrapping her arms tight around her neck. "You're okay!" Tears spring to her eyes and she doesn't even bother to try to hold them back. She has been so scared.

"We thought for sure the Doctor took you away!" Ellie rushes forward, falling on her sister with similar enthusiasm.

"She didn't do terrible experiments on you, did she?" Leah asks.

"No," Leni says. "She put an order out to have me killed, but I survived. Miss Bess saved me."

"I'll kill the Doctor," Ellie growls.

"We need to make a plan for that first," Leah says.

"I have so much to tell you," Leni says. "I've been outside in the world. I met the Source."

Leah gasps. "What? The Source is just out there, walking around like a normal person?"

"Not like a normal person. She was the one who was leading the team sent to kill me," Leni says.

"I'll kill the Source, too," Ellie says.

"You will not," Leni says. "Don't you dare, Ellie, do you hear me?"

Ellie sticks out her lower lip in a pout as she bends down to search the guard's pockets. She pulls his stun baton off his belt, making a pleased sound as she slaps it against her palm. "We need to get out of here. How did you get in, Leni?"

"There's a tunnel built into the air-filtration room that leads to an emergency exit into the desert," Leni says. "It's the same way we're getting out. But you have to promise me first, Ellie: You won't hurt Yelena."

"Is the Source with you?" Leah asks, almost bouncing with excitement.

"You brought her here?" Ellie asks, eyebrows scrunching together in anger.

"Yes, she helped me get here. And Yelena isn't bad," Leni says, trying to appeal to Ellie, who frowns deeply, but Leah just looks like she can't wait to meet her. "She didn't kill me. She's had plenty of opportunities. She keeps stopping herself. She's just . . . well, she's kind of dumb when it comes to actually feeling her feelings. I don't think *she* knows why she keeps saving me instead of killing me."

"Are you sure she's the Source, then?" Leah asks. "The Source is supposed to be smart."

"She's supposed to be perfect," Ellie says with eye-rolling mockery. She hands Leah the guard's knife and Leni his tranquilizer gun. "We've got to go."

"Get the smoke bomb, we might need it," Leah directs Ellie, who rushes over to get it, along with a teddy bear she's hollowed out into a makeshift backpack of supplies.

Leni peeks into the hall, looking both ways before she urges her sisters out of the playroom and into the corridor. "Hurry!" They stick close to the wall as they move toward the tunnels. Every turn they take down the maze that makes up the underground facility, Leni is sure the Doctor or the Director will appear, but the facility is strangely empty. Their footsteps echo hollowly, no alarms blaring, no guards shouting for help.

Maybe if Leni hadn't spent so many days with the forever suspicious Yelena, she would write it off. But now she can't ignore the creeping awareness that something isn't quite right.

Yelena is all about listening to your gut. And Leni's gut is screaming a warning at her.

"Wait," she whispers, throwing out an arm to stop Leah from walking past her.

"Footsteps!" Ellie hisses. "Someone's coming!" She grabs Leah's arm, dragging her back as Leni rushes down the hall with them, looking around desperately for a hiding spot.

"In here," Ellie says, pointing toward the air vent set low into the wall. She pries the vent cover free, urging

Leah and Leni inside. They barely fit. "Stay here until I get back."

Before Leni can protest, Ellie's slammed the air vent cover back in place and dashed out of sight, just as the footsteps grow louder and come into view through the slats in the cover. Since it doesn't sound like anyone's running after Ellie, she must have gotten out of sight just in time.

Leah sucks in a soft breath as the Doctor's heels pause in front of the air vent, accompanied by the shiny oxford shoes of a taller man. When he speaks, Leni recognizes the voice: the Director.

Her stomach burns like she's applied acid gum to her belly button. She wants to tear out of the air vent and rip his face off like a drop bear.

"The cameras should come back on in a few minutes," the Doctor says. "You know, if we had better funding, these power fluctuations wouldn't happen."

"The fact that you're angling for more money when you've made this kind of cross-country mess is stunning," the Director tells her.

"You agreed to the elimination of the Heart Subject," the Doctor says.

"And then you lost her before that could happen! I'm seriously considering scrapping the entire thing."

Leah stiffens next to Leni. Leni presses her hand against Leah's knee, trying to comfort her. *It's going to be okay*, she thinks. *I can't wait for you to see the rest of the world.*

Leah is going to love the world. And the library. She's going to lose her mind over the library. And Yelena made it sound like there were even *bigger* libraries than the one they went to.

But Leni has to get her out of here first. No one is going to stop her. Not the Doctor or the Director or even Yelena.

"You will not end this experiment," the Doctor says coldly. "It is not even up for discussion."

"You forget who's in charge," the Director says. "Now, if you'll—"

There's an electrical shudder in the air, and the lights around them flicker, like the entire building is coming back to full power.

"Finally," the Doctor says. But her relief is momentary. A split second later, the proximity alarms begin to blare, red lights flashing, signaling a security breach.

The Doctor whips her radio from her waist. "I need eyes on the subjects!" the Doctor barks into the radio.

Leah tenses next to her in the air vent as the Doctor's heels click even closer and then pause as the radio crackles to life: "No eyes on them! No eyes!"

"Have you actually lost another one? All of them?" the Director asks.

More alarms begin to blare. Blue lights suddenly accompanying the red ones. Leni knows what that means.

"This is your fault!" the Doctor rages at him, before her heels speed away and his feet follow down the hall. "Someone has tripped our outside security censors. If the Source has followed you here, the ramifications it will have on the experiment are immeasurable."

Leni smiles.

"What are you so happy about?" Leah hisses. "We're stuck in here! The cameras are back on! They'll see us if we sneak out."

"Yelena's here," Leni whispers. "She'll help."

"How can you be sure?" Leah asks.

"I can feel it," Leni says.

27.
HOME BASE

LOCATION: ARIZONA
OBJECTIVE: SAVE LENI

It takes much too long for the paralytic to wear off. Agonizing minutes stretch, Yelena's mind racing through horror scenarios as she tries desperately to wiggle her toes, her fingers, her nose, *anything*.

Her sensation and muscle control come back in bits and pieces. First a tingling in her palms, then she can blink one eye, then both. By the time she struggles to sit up, her mouth is dry, her eyes and skin gritty with sand blowing over her for those long minutes, and her mood? *Irate* is a good word for it.

Leni's tracks are still there, leading toward wherever the secret trapdoor she described is. Yelena follows, each step making her madder and madder. Half a mile and suddenly the tiny tracks disappear, and Yelena falls to her knees, scrabbling in the sand, searching the ground for the keypad.

Her hands hit metal. She pushes deeper, her fingers hooking around a metal ring. A few more seconds of scrabbling in the sand and she's found the keypad. She enters the code and heaves the trapdoor up, hydraulics kicking in to aid the heavy door as soon as it's triggered. Otherwise it would take two people to lift, at least.

A green glow emanates from the shaft below. Metal stairs are set into the wall, leading down into the space that opens up into what looks like a long tunnel or corridor.

Yelena doesn't hesitate, but she does take a bracing gulp of air as she descends into the facility that Leni used to call home. She's got nothing but her bracelets, but all she really needs is herself. Or at least that's what she's telling herself, because she is breaking into what she assumes is a highly guarded, highly armed situation.

It's oddly quiet as she gets to the bottom of the shaft and peeks out into a large room designed for air filtration. Yelena creeps around the tubes, heading to the door. But as soon as her foot crosses the threshold of the door, alarms begin to blare, blue lights flashing everywhere.

"Well, I guess they'll know I'm coming," Yelena mutters, squaring her shoulders and picking up her speed as she jogs down the corridor, taking a left and freezing as she comes face-to-face with the barrel of a gun.

"I've been looking for you," Director Cady says.

"I cannot say the same," Yelena says. "Which is rather ironic, considering I spent my first few weeks at the

Outpost wanting nothing more than to track your every move."

The tranquilizer gun is trained on her. She knows that even with her speed and agility, she won't be able to dodge a dart coming from this close a range.

He's caught her. She can't let him knock her out, which means playing his game. Letting him think she's defeated.

He should know better. A Widow is only defeated when she's stopped breathing. And sometimes not even then.

"We can do this the easy way, if you cooperate," he says. "Just hold out your wrists and I'll take you to an interrogation room. We can talk. No torture."

"How kind of you," Yelena says, dripping sarcasm, but she holds out her wrists. He tuts, gesturing for her to turn and adjust her arms *behind* her back. She tries not to roll her eyes as she does so. Either way, she's getting out of those cuffs. It doesn't matter if her arms are bound in front of her or behind.

He secures her and then pushes her between her shoulder blades to make her move.

"I didn't think you'd come here," Director Cady says as they make their way down the corridor. Yelena peers into the windows of the doors they pass, desperately searching for any sign of Leni. But every room is empty.

When the Director stops in front of one and opens it with his key card, she notes what pocket he tucks it into. She's going to need to take that off him.

She obediently lets him usher her inside. He shoves her too hard into the uncomfortable metal chair, his hand's grip telling her that under his calm surface lies a much angrier man.

Yelena hasn't just messed with his plans. She's put them in danger of being exposed. She's almost sure of it: Headquarters has no idea about Alexander Cady's cloning operation. The Doctor's experiment is too inefficient. Commander Starkovsky would never approve of such a thing.

But she wants confirmation from Cady's own lips before she gets out of here. She wants to be sure. So much of the past few days has mixed her head and her heart up, like they are comparable organs when she knows they aren't. That they can't be.

"I thought for sure, a clever girl like you, you'd be contacting S.H.I.E.L.D. or arranging a trade with one of our enemies. . . . After all, a Belova clone . . . that's worth something. Especially in the hands of the Source herself."

"Why did you do this?" Yelena demands shakily. She has to know. There has to be a reason beyond this badly thought out experiment by the Doctor.

"How could I not?" Director Cady asks. "As soon as you arrived at the Red Room, there were whispers about you. Your strength, your heart, your intelligence. I gambled on your potential, and look how it paid off. You grew up to be extraordinary. You exceeded all expectations."

"How did you do it?"

"It was simple, really, to steal the DNA needed. You bribe the right girls, the right staff workers, and suddenly, I have enough hair strands to create my own army. One that I control."

"Have I seemed easy to control so far?" Yelena asks. "Original me, or the little clones of me?"

His mouth twitches, belying his claims.

"Because the one I've been hanging out with is kind of a pain in the butt," Yelena continues, watching his face. "She ate all the hot cheese puffs, and she lectured me every time I stole a minivan. It would seem your Doctor instilled empathy and some sort of moral compass in her instead of *stripping* her of such a thing like you would for any good spy. What in the world were you thinking, letting that woman dictate your experiment?"

"You don't know what you're talking about," Director Cady says. "In fact, the Heart Subject wouldn't even exist without my suggestion. Dr. Chambers wanted to solely focus on the mind and body. I requested there be a third focused on the heart."

"Oh, so you're responsible for all the crying and moralizing in my life the past few days," Yelena says. "Are you bad at spycraft or something? You made Leni so heartfelt she'll do anything to protect the people she loves. And then you made the monumental mistake of *giving her sisters*. Do you even understand what you've made her capable of?"

"She'll be secured," Director Cady says with chilling certainty. Yelena's fists curl behind her back. She needs to get out of these cuffs.

"The Heart Subject will adjust back home just fine," Director Cady says. "We'll wipe her memories. She won't remember being taken out of the facility or making contact with the Source."

Yelena doesn't have time to examine the churn in her chest at the idea of Leni forgetting about their road trip. About *Yelena*.

She's up on her feet before she can even stop herself. She's got no control over her body for a moment.

"Sit. Down." He practically growls it. Yelena is not impressed, but she obeys. She understands men like him: They like to talk once they have someone who knows the truth.

They love to tell their secrets because they're so eager to show the world how smart they are. And human cloning at this level is very impressive, Yelena will give him that.

"I expected a lot when I heard you were arriving for your little exchange trip," Director Cady says. "I expected you to wipe the floor with my trainees, for instance, and you did. Repeatedly. Though I could've done without all the broken fingers and limbs."

"Crystal is very breakable in general," Yelena says. "It's in her name."

"She may be breakable, but she's no traitor," Director Cady says, placing his hands on the table in a stern, father-knows-best sort of way. Yelena barely resists rolling her eyes. She's never responded well to fatherly authority. "You know how the Commander feels about traitors. Do you think he'll let you keep any of your teeth? Your fingernails? Or perhaps he'll scoop out your memories completely and leave a husk to fill with fresh ones. You are a useful body, after all, even if we have to rebuild your brain and training from scratch."

Yelena's skin crawls, not just with his words, but with the awareness that before Leni, they wouldn't have bothered her as much. She would've just nodded along.

Instead, she's rejecting it with her whole body. The body that he is trying to reduce her to.

But she isn't just a body. Her memories . . . her training . . . her thoughts and experiences . . . those are the things that make her *her*. She is capable of amazing things. Of so much more than she realized. The proof is somewhere in this facility, tucked away in three girls who had formed the thing that she always lacked: a family.

"I thought the Cranes were exaggerating when they told me how much trouble you were," Director Cady says.

"Sometimes those two do get it right," Yelena says. "Like a broken clock."

"I expected trouble from you, of course. I knew you were sent by the Commander to infiltrate the Outpost. But I hadn't realized you'd been sent to derail my experiment. How did he find out? How long have you known about your clones?"

Yelena smiles, so slow that it times perfectly with the dawning of realization on his face.

"So your little cloning operation . . . it *was* unsanctioned by the Red Room. I wondered."

He pales, realizing what he's given away.

"I thought they must know in order for you to have my DNA. I understand wanting to create more of me. I am incredible, after all. But I kept getting hung up on the idea of the Commander wasting his time trying to create versions of me that cried more than they killed.

He wouldn't do that. But someone like you, who thought he could create better Widows than the Commander himself . . . you *would* do that. Do you enjoy it, being in this one-person competition with a leader so superior to you? You are a speck of dust on his shoe, Director Cady. A thief, a liar, and a traitor. And you know how the Commander feels about those. After all, you were just telling me about it."

"It doesn't matter," he says. "I have you. The Commander never has to find out about the girls."

"What are you going to do? Keep them locked up in this desert bunker forever?" Yelena asks.

"If it's in the best interest of the experiment, yes."

No. Just like Leni said when facing her down behind the sand dune. It's a rejection Yelena can feel down to her bones.

Her right wrist rotates in the cuffs, her fingers scrabbling against her sleeves where the final piece of acid gum is tucked.

"And what are you going to do with me?" Yelena asks.

Director Cady shrugs. "I suppose I'll keep you here, too. It's not like I can let you go, Belova."

She slips the gum free of the wrapper, wrapping it awkwardly around the first link of the chain that joins the metal cuffs together behind her back.

"It won't be so bad," Director Cady says. "You're

right, the Heart Subject introduced the idea of sisters to the group, much to the Doctor's disapproval. But the damage is done. You can be positioned as a big sister. A role model of sorts. If you behave yourself. And you *will*. Or there will be consequences."

"Do you really think you can do anything to me that will matter? I've been trained to withstand every kind of torture."

He smiles, a bland, managerial smile that sends chills down her spine at how sinister it feels paired with his words: "But your clones haven't."

Ice in her belly. Fire in her heart. It consumes her. She jerks the cuffs apart and leaps across the table, going straight for his throat. He's not expecting it. He's been so sure she was restrained. He should've known better.

They collide in a body-slamming rush as his chair tilts backward and he falls to the ground, Yelena's hands closing around his throat and squeezing.

"If you touch them I will end you, do you hear me?" She's babbling threats at him, completely out of control, the idea of Leni trapped in a room somewhere with an operative who's been trained in torture rushing through her head, filling her vision with a red haze.

She's not even sure what happens next. All she knows is that when her vision clears and she snatches her hands from his throat, he's not . . .

Did she kill him? Horror lances through her, a curious emotion when she knows she's better off if he is. She presses under his ear, searching for a pulse, and there's a part of her that's relieved to find it and a part of her that whispers *You need to finish it.*

What stops her is one thought: Leni wouldn't like it. She'd annoy Yelena for *hours* about it. Maybe even days. She is going to have to deal with enough whining from all three once she escapes this hellhole with them.

So instead, she searches his pockets—and locates the key card he used to open the interrogation room. She grabs it and is out the door in seconds.

28.
HOME BASE

LOCATION: ARIZONA
OBJECTIVE: FIND LENI AND HER SISTERS

Leni will go straight to her sisters. That Yelena knows for sure. Where are they?

Every hallway looks the same. Cement walls, flickering lights, doors leading to sterile-looking rooms when she gets them open.

She picks a direction, no strategy or reason, just a split-second decision. Racing down the corridor, she spots a door ahead. But when she slaps the key card she stole off Director Cady against it, it doesn't open. She slams her fist against the door, waiting a beat to see if there's a response. When there is none, she moves on to the next. Two more locked doors, two more seemingly empty rooms. She's about to check the third when a splintering sound—like glass cracking—jerks her attention down the corridor where it cuts left.

"Leni!" she yells, throwing all thoughts of stealth out the window as she runs toward the sound. Skidding around the corner, she spots her at the end of the long hall, and for a moment, it's like the cement walls are closing in on Yelena, because all she can see is Leni standing there, her little hands curled into fists, a security guard three times her size looming over her.

Just for a moment. Then her brain catches up with what she's seeing. Leni wasn't wearing a white shirt—her shirt was blue—so this . . . this is . . .

"Give that back to me, you toad!" screams the girl, delivering a well-placed kick to the man's knee with the force of a much taller girl. He falls back much harder than he should, considering how small she is.

This must be the clone focused on strength of body over everything else. Hopefully she won't cry as much as her sister.

The man's leg buckles at Ellie's roundhouse, and she's already dancing back as he falls forward, delivering another kick to his head to make sure he's unconscious before immediately going to strip him of his weapons.

Yelena steps toward her, and Ellie's head whips up. A strand of blond hair—tinged red with blood—drops across her button nose, and she blows at it, irritated.

"My sister said the Source was around," says the girl, looking her up and down with none of the fear Leni had when she first realized Yelena was the grown-up version of herself. "Is that really what I'm going to look like?" She sounds unimpressed, and Yelena would be insulted, but she knows she's very pretty. Vanity has nothing to do with it. It's one of the reasons the Red Room chose her. Beauty is a useful tool.

"You must be Ellie," Yelena says.

Ellie yanks a stun baton off the guard, making a pleased sound when she presses the button and an electric crackle fills the air, blue light sparking off the end. "That's me." She levels the baton straight at Yelena, her head tilting. "Are you here to stop me or help me? Leni says you're kind of dumb. That you don't know what you want." Ellie makes a disgusted sound. "You're *old* and you don't even know something as simple as that? I knew what I wanted when I was *six*."

"How wise of you," Yelena says, changing her mind about liking this clone. "Where are your sisters, by the way?" She prays Leni hasn't run into the Doctor. If they can just get back through the tunnel, Yelena can get them out of here. To where, she has no idea. But she'll come up with something once they're out in the desert and free of this spooky, sterile place.

"My sisters are safe," Ellie says. "You didn't answer my question."

Yelena lets out a nervous laugh, because Ellie has not put down the stun gun and it's a nasty one. She can tell. And unfortunately, because it's a baton, it's long enough that Ellie can take Yelena out before she could grab her and stun her with her Widow's Bite.

Getting your clones to cooperate with you in escape instead of knocking them unconscious is a lot more difficult, but she can't exactly pull three eight-year-olds out of here on her own steam without creating some sort of litter to drag them. And there is nowhere near enough time to do that.

The more time they spend down here, the more chances they have to run into the Doctor. Yelena looks toward the corner, where a camera glints. Is the Doctor watching even now?

She can't resist. She gestures to the kid and then to the camera like, *Really, you had to clone me and make her as vicious as a poked hog?*

"Can you just bring me to Leni?" she asks Ellie. "You can keep that thing on me the whole time if it makes you feel better. But the three of you are going to need this"—she pulls out the key card she took off Director Cady—"to get through any of the doors. So you might as well bring me along."

"Maybe I should just take it off you," Ellie says.

"Try," Yelena says, infusing the word with all the threat she can muster. Which is a lot. This clone hits a bit too close to home.

"Maybe I will," Ellie says, but there's a lot less confidence in her voice.

"Your sister won't like it if I return with you maimed,

so I'd rather you not," Yelena says. "Did they make you stubborn on top of strong?"

"I can't *believe* Leni just blabbed to you about the experiment," Ellie mutters.

"And I can't believe such a silly experiment exists," Yelena says. For a moment, as Ellie moves forward, she thinks the girl is intent on attacking. But instead, she pushes past her, toward the north side of the facility. "By focusing you three so narrowly, the Doctor could never succeed with her goal. I at least was given a well-rounded education. You three were raised in individual little bubbles."

Ellie snorts. "Like I want to spend time reading books like Leah or talking about my feelings like Leni."

"Punching things is very satisfying, but some situations call for other tactics," Yelena says, trying not to sound like a schoolteacher and failing miserably.

"I prefer biting to punching," Ellie says, and then she grins, making sure to show her teeth. Is it Yelena's imagination, or are her incisors a little pointier than Yelena's had been at that age?

"Did you . . . did you *file* your teeth down?" Yelena demands.

Her smile turns smug and close-lipped. "The Doctor's stingy with weapons. I had to make myself into a better one."

"You have baby teeth still!" Yelena sounds like someone's disapproving older sister right now, marching after the bloody clone, but she can't help herself. She half wants to run into the Doctor so she can give the terrible woman a piece of her mind.

"And I'll file the big ones, too, when they grow in," Ellie says.

"Maybe we just get you a nice knife instead," Yelena says.

"Maybe a knife *and* a good tooth file? Mine was not a very good one."

Yelena kind of hates how *hopeful* she looks. "I'm not sure there's actually such a thing as a tooth file, but okay, you can have both. But we need to get out of here first, which means we need your sisters. That was Leni's whole deal: She wasn't leaving without any of you."

"Well, yeah, we're sisters," Ellie says, like it's that simple. Yelena supposes it is, for them. "Come on. But if you try anything funny, I'll zap you and then I'll bite you."

"You bite me, I'll bite you back," Yelena mutters, but Ellie just grins wider like she knows her threat's worse with those teeth.

29.
HOME BASE

LOCATION: ARIZONA
OBJECTIVE: RUN

"I think we need to try to make a run for it," Leni whispers to Leah in the air vent. It's been at least fifteen minutes since the alarms stopped blaring like someone shut them off and not one person has come down the corridor. Not even Ellie. "What if Ellie needs our help?"

Leah swallows, the air-vent cover casting striped shadows across her nervous face. "You're right," she whispers. "Let's go."

Leni pushes the vent cover free, climbing out first, her hands wary and at the ready, all too aware that the bracelets Yelena snapped on her are deadly. She hates that right now, she's grateful for the power of them. It makes her understand Yelena better. It makes her wonder if this is her future: becoming a deadly thing.

She never thought about the *why* behind her focus until Yelena told her to question it. And now all she can think of is why. Why would they want her to feel so deeply, if it means she hurts more when she understands more? She's seen her future in Yelena, and none of the tools that she's been told to carefully craft apply. It makes no sense.

Is that why they wanted me dead, because *I'm not deadly?*

"Leni!" Leah yells. "Duck!"

Leni flattens herself belly-first onto the ground as Leah chucks the smoke bomb over her. It hits the ground, skittering to the right, exploding in a cloud of purple smoke at the feet of the guard who was creeping behind Leni slowly and carefully. His stun baton clatters down as the smoke engulfs him and he descends into furious scratching everywhere the purple smoke touches.

"Run! Don't let the smoke near you!" Leah shouts, grabbing Leni's hand and dragging her down the hall, the smoke licking at their heels as it spreads. As they skid around the corner and head down the next hall, the hurried click of heels fills the air.

"She's here," Leah whispers, looking around frantically. But there's no air vent to hide in this time. As the Doctor comes into sight at the end of the hall, she pauses, drinking them in.

"You've returned," she says, her gaze settling on Leni.

Leah tries to step protectively in front of her sister, but Leni holds her back. She stands tall, meeting the Doctor's gaze unflinchingly. She's still scared of her—Leni knows too much not to be—but she won't shrink like a plant in the desert.

"I've come for my sisters," Leni says. "We're leaving."

"You're not leaving," the Doctor says. "You are proprietary scientific property."

"I'm a person," Leni says, and instead of stepping away from the Doctor, she steps forward with each word. She knows what she has to do. "I'm a sister. I'm a reader. I like spicy food and books about sisters and world records. And, yeah, okay, I'm a clone. But I don't belong to you. None of us do."

She's so close to the Doctor now. She could reach out and touch her. She kind of wants to poke her. Just to see how she likes it. But she has to prepare herself to do so much more.

She has to do what Yelena would do.

The Doctor's throat bobs when her eyes fall on the bracelets on Leni's wrists.

"Do you know what these are?" Leni asks.

The Doctor nods.

"Yelena set them up for me," Leni says. "I'm pretty sure that if I use them they'll dispense a shock charge so high that it will kill a person." She tilts the bracelets just so. The Doctor's eyes remain transfixed. "Do you want to find out?"

"You wouldn't," the Doctor says, trying to sound confident. "You are much too sensitive to kill someone. It's not in the programming we've given you."

"This isn't about programming," Leni says. "This is about *her* nature. My nature. I know exactly where I come from now. Who I come from. And Yelena . . . Yelena would never leave you alive. Not when you pose a threat. Isn't that what you are? A threat to my sisters?"

"Stop using that word," the Doctor says.

"You can't make her do anything. That's what I've learned, the last few days in her company."

Leni almost jumps as Yelena's voice rings out. Ellie follows behind her, clutching a stun baton and looking none too pleased to be in the Source's presence. There's blood all over Ellie's chin. Leni's relieved and then alarmed when she realizes that it's not Ellie's.

Yelena moves slowly and surely down the hall, a tranquilizer gun in her hand pointed dead at the Doctor's chest. Leni wants to sag in relief; she won't have to hurt the Doctor. She can step back and let Yelena take over.

But can she? The thought lurks in her heart. Can she trust Yelena, really?

"You okay?" Yelena asks her.

Leni nods. "Have you . . ."

"Recovered from you stabbing me with a paralytic

and abandoning me in the desert? Yeah. All good now. I can wiggle all my fingers and my toes. See?" She drums her fingers along the barrel of the tranquilizer gun, the muzzle just half a foot from the Doctor's face now.

"Are you mad at me?" Leni asks.

"We'll discuss it when we're not threatening our enemies," Yelena says.

"So you *are* mad," Leni says.

"What if I had gotten eaten by buzzards?" Yelena asks. "They're like the drop bears of the desert, you know. Now scoot."

Leni obeys as Yelena swings into place so all three girls are behind her, tucked firmly out of reach of the Doctor.

Even in the chaos, the Doctor's white jacket and neat French twist are pristine—except for a spray of blood across the hem. It almost looks decorative at this angle.

"You're shorter than I thought you'd be," the Doctor says, looking Yelena up and down, finally examining the Source up close for the first time.

"Sorry to disappoint," Yelena says. She doesn't like the unsettling way the woman looks at her, hungry for information.

"Not disappointment," the Doctor says. "Just an observation."

Yelena casts a glance over her shoulder to make sure

the girls are safely shielded by her body. The Doctor's going to have to go through her to get to them.

"Your security is severely lacking. I counted . . . what, only six guards in total?"

"My budget has been severely lacking," the Doctor says sourly. "And we've never had much reason to worry about infiltration until now."

"Confidence is killer," Yelena says. "So is under-funding. I'm assuming that Director Cady is siphoning Outpost budgets for this little venture, which makes it a trickle of money, not a stream."

"I'm not sure why you care."

"Just confirming suspicions," Yelena says. "I'm taking the girls, by the way. Consider your experiment officially over. Before you follow us, I advise you to check your storage room. You'll see what Ellie and I got up to with what was left of your security guards. Then think about if you want that to happen to your face."

Behind her Ellie grins, showing her bloody teeth and flexing her muscles. The Doctor steps back slightly, smoothing a hand over her hair and then her ear.

"You just got here," the Doctor says, trying to buy time. "I have so many questions. You are the Source, after all."

"My answers would not please you," Yelena says.

"Girls, stay behind me," she orders when she feels Ellie tense next to her.

The Doctor's face twitches. "Don't call them that."

"What?" Yelena asks, baffled. "Girls?"

The Doctor crosses the space between them in three steps. Yelena has to snap her arm out, slapping it against the woman's sternum to stop her when she's just inches away.

"They are not *girls*. They are *subjects*," the Doctor hisses.

Yelena's head tilts. She breathes in and out. There's so much she could say here. So much rage she could unleash or truth she could tell. But she settles on the coldest, hardest truth.

"You're an idiot," she says, and head-butts her as hard as she can.

Leni shrieks as Ellie lets out a cackle of delight and Leah a startled gasp.

Pain lances through her head, but Yelena can bear it. She never makes a move she hasn't thought through. Well, except for that time she decided to save her own clone that turned into saving her own *clones*. But she's giving herself a pass on that one. It's been that kind of week.

The Doctor blinks, stunned after the collision of skull and skin. Blood trickles down her forehead. She staggers a step backward, teetering on her heels, and for a moment, it almost looks like she'll recover instead of black out from the blow.

Yelena tenses, ready to deliver the final hit, but before she can, Leni dashes forward and with one finger pokes the Doctor in the stomach.

The Doctor topples back like a rag doll, sprawling on the floor totally unconscious.

"Get her key card!" Yelena directs. Leni grabs it, brandishing it at Yelena, who takes it.

"Let's go!" Leni says.

"Hold on to each other," Yelena urges, ushering them forward, the precious key card clutched in her fingers. They race down the corridor, the empty echoes of their pounding feet the only sound. Ahead of them, two giant iron doors. They're so close—just feet away from the doors leading to outside—when . . .

"BELOVA!" a voice roars down the corridor.

It's Director Cady. She should've set her Widow's Bites to *kill*. Spending so much time with Leni has made her soft. If she went on a road trip with Ellie instead, they probably would've left a trail of bodies behind instead of stealing a few minivans and tote bags.

"Go!" Yelena says, swiping the card against the key slot. The light turns from red to green, and Ellie pushes against the doors as Director Cady limps toward them.

"Run for the mechanic shed! Get in one of the dune buggies!"

The desert is blue-black at night, the stars above brilliant and shining in a place with so little light pollution. The three girls run, their feet sinking and struggling through the sand as Yelena pushes the doors closed right in Director Cady's face. She's got both his key card and the Doctor's. He'll have to take the emergency exit out or find a way to override the system to get out the main way.

The doors thump as someone throws their body against them from the inside.

Or he could throw a fit and do that. Yelena shrugs. It's not her problem anymore.

She races across the sand, the mechanic shed coming into sight as headlights flick on in the distance. Before she can call out, a dune buggy rears out of the shed opening, Leah behind the wheel. The buggy screeches up to Yelena, her three clones packed together tight.

"I'll drive," Yelena says, and Leah pouts a little, but she scoots over to sit on Leni's lap while Ellie takes the back seat to guard their rear. Ellie's found a wrench as a makeshift weapon and keeps slapping it against her palm. It is not an entirely un-menacing sight. "Good job, finding a weapon," Yelena tells her, and is rewarded with another bloody smile.

She has a rough idea that the town they passed over

is to the east, so she points the dune buggy that way and floors it.

"We should've blown the place up," she hears Ellie mutter as they speed across the sand, kicking up grit that stings her eyes the faster they go.

The more distance they put between them and the bunker, the more Yelena can't help but agree with Ellie.

She should've cleansed that place with fire. Left nothing but ashes behind.

Leaving survivors . . . that just spells trouble.

30.
THE SLEEPY HOLLOW MOTEL

LOCATION: ARIZONA
OBJECTIVE: FIGURE OUT A NEW LIFE . . . FAST.

By the time the expanse of sand turns to rough road and then asphalt, the sun is peeking across the sky. The first glimpse Leah and Ellie have of real civilization is the Sleepy Hollow Motel, the ancient neon sign of an owl blinking on and off in the fuzzy morning light.

It's the kind of place that's perfect to hide out in—the type of motel where people don't ask questions and everyone pays in cash. Yelena walks up to the front desk with her three sand-streaked and exhausted clones trailing after her, and the man behind it doesn't even flinch at the sight of them.

"One room," Yelena says, digging out some cash stolen from the first van and hidden in her boot, handing it over in exchange for a key. Without another word, she hustles the girls across the parking lot and into room twenty-three, making note of the vending machines at the end of the row of doors.

She unlocks the door and ushers them inside. After

checking the bathroom and under the beds, she gives Leni a nod. "I'll be right back."

Raiding the vending machines takes a good ten minutes. She's tense the entire time, half expecting Director Cady or the Doctor to come speeding into the parking lot, followed by Johanna's team.

She hopes they're okay. That they're not being punished too much for failing their mission. Director Cady was hypocritical enough to blame them when he failed to keep hold of her, too.

When she gets back to the room, she finds all three girls have grouped themselves on the queen bed farthest from the door, pillows strewn on the ground. There's an eerie calm in the room, like the shock of the night has finally settled in.

"Anyone hungry?" Yelena asks, trying to go for normal. They need to eat, rest, and then steal another car and get on the road. To where, she isn't sure. She's going to have to figure it out.

Yelena dumps the contents of the vending machine on the bed. Leni smiles weakly at her when she sees the array of food, but the other two eye it cautiously.

"Did you poison it?" Ellie asks.

"Check the seals," Yelena says, instead of taking the bait. Leah laughs as she grabs a bag of hot corn puffs.

"Those are good," Leni says. "They're spicy,"

"Is this what you've been eating this whole time?" Ellie asks, making no move toward any of the snacks. She keeps her back to the wall, her body angled toward the door and window like she wants to be prepared. Ellie's got one eye on Yelena at all times. She's tempted to do a routine to track the girl's reflexes. Are they as good as hers were at that age? Or better, because strength and fighting are her focus?

"It's good," Leni says softly, but she seems to wilt under Ellie's wary disdain.

Yelena is starting to see a clearer picture of the sisters. Ellie is the leader. She's not surprised that Leni is more of a follower. But Leah's quiet personality does surprise her. She expected the intelligence-focused clone to be quick-witted and never stop talking, but she seems to be quite the opposite. A girl overly cautious with her words.

But maybe that's what happened when the knowledge of her captivity grew with her lessons and intelligence.

Yelena just smiles as Ellie glares at her. "We'll introduce them to hot sauce once we're back on the road," Yelena tells Leni. "I'll be right back." She gives the girl a short nod, checking to make sure the door is locked *and* barricaded, before she ducks inside the bathroom.

The girls need some time alone to reconnect away from prying eyes—even hers.

She leans her forehead against the closed door, breathing deep, trying to calm the uneasy thrum under her skin. As much as she'd love to wash away the grit and sweat that cling to her, she's not risking keeping the clones out of her sight that long. Leah's smart—she could probably turn the vending-machine food into a bomb. And Yelena would be foolish to trust Ellie. There's a certain look in Ellie's eyes, like she's seen too much in that hellish bunker the Doctor thinks is an adequate home in which to raise perfection. But Yelena suspects it's much more than that: Learning how to break free changed her.

It changed all three of them. It changed Yelena.

But Leni is resilient. That much Yelena knows. Her sisters must be, too. There's just so little she knows about the other two. She can learn. She must learn, she realizes with a sick jolt.

She's all they have.

How did she get here? She's asked herself that countless times throughout the past days. Every time she hasn't had an answer.

She hasn't wanted to admit the truth.

Every choice she's made, it's been to protect Leni like she herself should've been protected.

Her fingers curl against the door into fists, her body tries to reject the thought, but the truth's there in her mind. It's been driven into Yelena's heart like a spike by that tiny, sticky hand that she had to keep swatting so Leni wouldn't accidentally eat acid gum.

A handful of days with her clone, that's all it took to undo it. The years of being broken down in training, of subliminal messaging, of brainwashing.

Because that is what it was. She can see the wrong of it now, and it hurts to know that it didn't matter enough when it was just her, but it means something that it matters when it's Leni and her sisters.

She was told she is worthless. That only the Red Room gives her worth.

But the truth is right there on the other side of the door: She isn't worthless. She is so valuable, so gifted, she has such amazing potential that they *cloned* her.

Those girls eating hot corn puffs and peanut butter cups only exist because she scored too high on tests and trials she didn't even know she was taking, but she should've known. Life is a test when you belong to the Red Room.

Even the most brainwashed of Widows couldn't ignore the reality that led her here, to this moment, to these sisters.

They would only clone the best of the best. Which means she is the very best. And that's dangerous knowledge to have.

There's a knock at the bathroom door. It sends vibrations through Yelena's forehead.

"Yelena?" says a small voice. "Are you okay?"

"I'm fine, Leni. I'll be right out."

But she can't leave this bathroom until she has some sort of plan. She took them, they're free—for now. But that could last anywhere from four minutes to forever.

The choices before her are grim. She has no connections in this country except the Outpost and the Order of Minerva. The Outpost wants to kill her, and when she reached out to the Order of Minerva, they led her to an abandoned farmhouse with a member of the Order buried in the front yard. That sends a certain kind of message, in Yelena's opinion.

She's on her own. The feeling creeps over her. The Commander always told her a spy must float above. They are creatures of solitude. *Lonely is an art, little bird.*

Yelena opens the bathroom door a crack to check on the girls. They're sitting on the bed farthest from the door, their knees touching, the pile of junk food in the neat triangle they've formed.

Lonely may very well be an art. But sisterhood is a masterpiece.

※

"I don't want to get down!" Leah protests, bouncing even harder on the bed. Yelena is sincerely regretting buying those candy bars. Leni has never gotten *this* sugar-high before.

"But you have to," Yelena says.

"You're supposed to be cooler than this," Leah says, stomping her feet across the pillows as she finally ceases the incessant bouncing that's been going on for twenty minutes.

Yelena's temples ache. Her head is threatening to pound like the rest of her bruised and still slightly sandy body. She can't remember the last time she slept. Ellie's sacked out on the love seat, and Yelena wonders if they all got her ability to sleep through anything. The Red Room trained that out of her—a sound sleeper is one who gets knifed.

"You should rest" is all she says to Leah. "You've had a long day."

"I'm not tired," Leah says, but the huge yawn that follows gives her away. Her cheeks grow pink as Leni giggles. "Shut up," she mutters.

"Gaining sudden freedom from a desert bunker you were rarely allowed to leave would make anyone a little giddy," Yelena says. "But we've got a long drive ahead of us tomorrow, so you should sleep."

"Where are we going?" Leni asks.

I have no idea.

"Canada," Yelena says brightly, like it's a sure thing. "Maybe we'll learn how to make maple syrup."

Leni folds her arms across her chest and quirks her pale eyebrows. "You don't sound very sure."

"That's because I'm not," Yelena says.

Leni bites her lip. It sends warning bells clanging through Yelena's head. That's her tell.

"You have a secret," Yelena says, trying to sound coaxing instead of accusing and failing just a little.

"Promise you won't get mad," Leni says.

"Is it something that's going to help us? Then I won't get mad."

"And if it's not?"

"I don't care, Leni, just tell me."

"Miss Bess made me memorize a phone number along with the back-door code. Just in case we got separated."

Yelena's eyes widen at the implication. "Do you mean you've had a way to contact the Order of Minerva this whole time and you've let me run around Kansas, fight my friends, and destroy world-record-holding balls of twine instead of just giving me the phone number?"

"I didn't trust you, and you proved me right! You were just bringing me back to turn me in to save your skin. What did you say? You lost your mind a little the first time you saw me? I bet you regretted saving me the second our feet hit the sidewalk."

"Sooner," Yelena says, and Leni's eyes widen like she expected her to argue. "I won't lie to you anymore." She's acutely aware that both Leah and Ellie, whom Leah shook awake, are watching them raptly. "So here's the truth, for all of you: I have no allies here and a giant target on my back. I've got enough money for a tank of gas and maybe three more meals before we have to start stealing. We're on our own unless we reach out to Bess and the Order of Minerva. I can't promise they'll help us. I can try . . . but only if you give me the number."

"You haven't been trustworthy at all," Ellie says.

"I got you out of that hole you grew up in," Yelena says. "If I hadn't been there, the Doctor would've gotten hold of one of you and used your love for each other to manipulate you into giving up."

"You don't know that," Leah says.

"Yes, I do," Yelena says. "The Doctor made many mistakes in her experiment. But the biggest one was letting you form bonds with each other and then find a word for it. She should've raised each of you in isolation from each other. But she didn't. She let you love each other, and love allows a person to manipulate you. Like I'm going to do right now with all three of you."

Ellie lets out a warning hiss that has Yelena thoroughly amused.

"It's not manipulation if you tell us you're manipulating us," Leni says.

"No, there's a lesson in it," Yelena says, and Leni swallows hard. "So learn it. I've been trying to teach you about the world and survival this whole time, little Leni. You have not listened well. I hope you will now. And so will your sisters. If you love each other, if you want to keep each other safe, you will call the Order of Minerva. I won't abandon you. You can flee with me. But I think that Leah has realized the problem with that choice."

Both the girls look at their sister, and Leah's chin tilts up stubbornly. "She belongs to the Red Room. She's nearly fully trained, which means she's valuable. And she's the Source for a reason. She's the best. They will not rest until their operative is returned. They will never stop chasing her. But the three of us . . . the Red Room doesn't know about us. The experiment was not sanctioned by Headquarters. It was the Director's secret project. Step one in his plan to shift power by creating better operatives in America."

"You *are* the smart one," Yelena says.

"You have no idea," Leah says. It is not said as a brag but instead as a world-weary fact. Her voice shouldn't be able to bear that heaviness at this age, yet it does.

Yelena isn't equipped for this. She's more of a threat to them the longer she stays with them.

"I still say we don't give her the number," Ellie says. "What if she hurts Miss Bess?"

"If I wanted to hurt Bess, I would've killed her in the penthouse. Instead, I knocked her out."

"I think we have to risk it," Leah says. "We need Miss Bess."

She and Leni look to Ellie, who sighs. "If you hurt Miss Bess, I'll tear your throat out," she tells Yelena.

"Understood," Yelena says, trying to sound amused, but feeling a little disturbed at how sincere Ellie's squeaky little voice sounds.

Leni goes over to the motel desk, scribbling a number on the pad of paper. She hands it to Yelena, but when Yelena takes it, she doesn't let go until Yelena meets her eyes.

"I'm trusting you," Leni says solemnly. "If you choose wrong again, Ellie won't need to tear your throat out. I'll do it myself."

Yelena swallows against the words that rise unbidden in her mind.

I'll do anything to keep that kind of darkness from touching her.

31.
THE SLEEPY HOLLOW MOTEL

LOCATION: ARIZONA
OBJECTIVE: MAKE CONTACT

Punching the number into the motel phone under three pairs of watchful eyes and Ellie's obvious bloodthirstiness is more than a little nerve-racking, but Yelena is a pro. She plays it cool as the phone rings three times before someone picks up.

"Hello?" a woman's voice says cautiously.

"Hello," Yelena says.

There's a distinct pause that tells Yelena that it wasn't the voice she was hoping to hear.

"Who is this?" the woman's voice asks. Yelena recognizes the clipped vowels from the encounter with Bess in the penthouse. "How did you get this number?"

"I believe we met in the hotel," Yelena says. "You were very surprised to see me."

There's a silence. "You weren't supposed to be there," Bess finally says.

"I guess it's good I was, isn't it?" Yelena asks. "You couldn't protect her."

"Is she . . ." Bess's voice cracks. "Please tell me she's okay."

"They're all okay," Yelena says.

"All of them . . . You . . ." The surprise hangs heavy on the line. "What did you do? How did you get them out? No—no. This is a trick," she says firmly. "You're lying."

Yelena rolls her eyes and holds out the phone. "Clone spawn, let the nice lady know you're all here with me and free from your underground clone lair."

"Hi, Miss Bess," Leni says.

"The Source hasn't murdered us, but she's *really* annoying," Ellie adds.

"She doesn't follow *any* rules, Miss Bess," Leah says.

"Rules are overrated," Yelena says. "Satisfied?" she asks into the phone.

There's a pause. "Where do you want to meet?"

"There's a diner on Main Street," Yelena says. "Can you meet me in the morning?"

"You're in Arizona still?"

"I'm sixteen and on the run with three tiny versions of me, forgive me for not hightailing it out of the state immediately without stopping to let them sleep and have some snacks. Do you *know* how much Leni eats?"

"Do you want me to come alone?" Bess asks.

"Show up alone or with your entire cabal of goddess-loving science types. I don't care. All I care is that someone actually shows this time."

"We left you what you needed in Kansas," Bess says.

"Leaving us the coordinates to the facility and expecting us to find it was a huge gamble," Yelena says. "You had no way of knowing I'd take her there. That I'd save any of them."

"Yes, I did," Bess says. "You forget, Yelena. I've spent the last eight years raising you. I know you."

A chill fizzes through her, leaving an ache everywhere it touches. "You know nothing," Yelena says. "I'll see you at the diner."

The Main Street Diner is not very creatively named, but the smell that hits as soon as Yelena walks inside is pure, greasy heaven. America really does know how to do diner food. And this one looks like it hasn't been updated since the 1950s. It has a checkerboard floor and red vinyl booths, neon signs scattered on the walls.

"Did they ever teach you about milkshakes?" Yelena asks as the girls get settled in a neat row in their booth. She takes the opposite side so that she can see the front door and anyone coming inside.

"Of course we know about milkshakes," Leah says scornfully. "They didn't feed us gruel or anything."

"Well, Leni didn't know about hot corn puffs, so I wouldn't put it past that Doctor of yours," Yelena says. She wonders how long it will be until the Doctor and Director Cady send out another team to find them. There may be one moving toward them right now.

But they need to eat, so she lets her clones order burgers, making sure to encourage them to add jalapeños, since they all seem to have inherited her love of spicy things.

"Are all restaurants like this?" Ellie asks after the waitress takes their order and then shouts it to the short-order cook in the back with the gravelly affection of a woman who's spent her life doing the exact same thing.

"This one's kind of old-school," Yelena says, watching as a car with tinted windows pulls up across the street. A woman in big sunglasses with a scarf wrapped over her hair gets out, walking briskly toward the diner. Yelena tenses, her hand going for the lipstick tube Leni used to paralyze her in the desert. Leni left it behind, not realizing there are a few doses left in it.

The woman walks inside, her eyes immediately going to the girls.

"Miss Bess!" Leah says, trying to climb over her sister to get to her.

"Girls!" Bess tears off the scarf and rushes toward them. Yelena readies the paralytic, just in case, but the woman falls to her knees in front of the booth and embraces the girls with a sob. They hug her back as she cries, relief in every single line of her face.

"I can't believe it," she says. "All three of you. I'd hoped and dreamed that someday— Look at you! Are you all okay?"

"We're fine," Leni says. "Yelena got us out."

"Well, she helped," Ellie says. "Leah created a smoke bomb that took one guard out."

"And Leni knocked another guard out!" Leah adds. "It was so cool."

"Even I was impressed," Ellie says.

"You're the one who took out the other guards while me and Leah hid," Leni points out.

"The Source helped with that," Ellie says. "But we got ourselves free first."

"I told you, she doesn't like it when you call her that," Leni says to Ellie, who rolls her eyes.

"Look, girls, the food's here," Yelena says as the waitress comes toward them with plates lining her arms. "Why don't you eat? Miss Bess and I are going to go over here and talk."

Bess wipes at her face with shaking hands as she straightens, letting Yelena guide her to the booth across from the girls, who fall upon the burgers with an adorable amount of enthusiasm. Yelena feels a little twinge of guilt that she's been filling them up on junk food for a whole day.

"How did you do it?" Bess asks.

"They helped," Yelena says simply. "Teamwork is key."

Bess lets out a laugh. "This is crazy," she says, staring at Yelena. "I can't believe I'm sitting in front of you. Before the penthouse, I never thought I'd ever meet you. At least, not . . ."

"The real me," Yelena says.

Bess nods.

"I need to know how far-reaching the Order of Minerva is," Yelena says. "Is it a dwindling group of scientists or do you have real resources and money behind you? The security guards I had to take out in the penthouse were the kind that required serious money. Does that mean you have enough to protect them?"

"We can protect them, if that's what you need to know," Bess says.

"Like you protected Leni from my strike team?" Yelena asks.

Bess flushes. "We were unprepared, I'll admit it. We were planning on removing all three girls at once. The

Doctor's decision to eliminate Leni took us by surprise. We were in a mad scramble to get her out. And then your arrival at the penthouse . . . I should've seen it coming. I should've taken her straight to the safe house we've already secured. I have it laid out for them, Yelena. An entire life in a remote, hard-to-access area, raised by people who love them and know them."

"People like you," Yelena says.

"The entire Order of Minerva is behind us," Bess says. "But yes, I will be one of their main caretakers. We've known them all their lives."

"You keep saying *us* and *we*," Yelena says.

Bess smiles gently and looks out the window, waving toward the car she got out of a few minutes ago. There's movement behind the tinted windows, and a dark-haired woman with cat-eye glasses gets out.

At the girls' table, Leni lets out a shaky gasp when she spots the woman heading across the street toward the diner. "Miss Irene!"

She bolts out of the booth, running toward the glass doors of the diner just as Irene comes bursting inside, a wide smile on her face.

"You faked her death?" Yelena asks Bess.

Bess nods. "So that she could set up Leni's new life without Director Cady or the Doctor being suspicious."

"That's dedication," Yelena says, watching as Leni tearfully brings Irene to the table with her sisters, the other two falling into overlapping conversation, trying to fill her in on all the things she's missed since she left.

"We are," Bess says, pulling Yelena's attention back. "Dedicated, I mean."

"To what, exactly?" Yelena asks carefully. "Because a whole secret society of scientists who want to take care of a trio of clones . . . well, some people might think that you have reasons other than you care for them and want them to have nice, normal lives. I heard how the Doctor referred to them. She snapped at me when I called them girls."

"She always insisted they were test subjects," Bess says. "She wanted to create distance between the handlers and the girls. Much to her chagrin, she couldn't control empathy. Irene and I joined the experiment as young scientists fresh out of college. We had no idea what we were getting into. By the time we did, we were in too deep."

"The Red Room does not let go of its disciples," Yelena says.

"It does not," Bess agrees. "Thus why we faked Irene's death."

"So, you'll run with the girls," Yelena says. "That's the plan? To give up your whole lives to hide in a safe house?"

"They *are* our lives," Bess says. "My plan is to take them to the new safe house and *live*. The Order of Minerva will destroy what is left of the Doctor's data. There are ways of ruining her that are much worse than death for a scientist like her."

"And Director Cady?" Yelena asks. "How do you plan on destroying him?"

"That's where you come in," says Irene, sliding into the booth next to Bess, taking her hand. Bess smiles, covering her hand with her own.

"I'd be happy to take care of Director Cady," Yelena says grimly.

"We *can* take you with us, Yelena," Bess says hesitantly. "We will house you and try to keep you safe. But we need to leave immediately. Staying any longer in a town so close to the bunker isn't a good idea."

"No, I can't come with you," Yelena says immediately. "The reason that I agreed to meet with you is because my presence in my clones' lives puts a target on their backs. If the Red Room finds out what Director Cady has done, we're in trouble."

The Commander would never let the girls go free. To train three of her as he wished . . . it's a golden opportunity that Director Cady and the Doctor squandered. The Commander will not.

But Yelena cannot bear a reality that holds that path. The path where the Commander takes hold of all three of them and strips Leni and her sisters of what makes them special and unique. He'd turn them into spies with holes where their hearts used to be, just like Yelena, and there would be no little clones of their own to fill that hole like Leni did for her.

The Commander would make them sisters of war, not sisters of the soul. She can't let that happen.

Which means she must let Leni go.

"I appreciate you being wise enough to see the truth of this situation," Irene says. "Wanting to run from what waits for you back in the Red Room would be natural."

"I am not a little girl who runs," Yelena says. "I will deal with Director Cady. If I decide the girls can go with you, he will not ever be bothering them again."

"Are you going to kill him?" pipes up a voice behind her. Yelena tilts her head up to see Leni peeking over the booth.

"I don't need to," Yelena says. "In fact, I need him to stay alive. Come here, I want to talk to you for a minute." She pats the spot next to her, and Leni slides out of her own booth and into Yelena's.

"We'll give you a minute," Bess says, as she and Irene join Leni's sisters at the next booth.

"You look like you had too much hot sauce," Leni says. "Are we gonna go now that Miss Bess and Miss Irene are here? We're all together, so we can go, right?"

"You're going to go," Yelena says. "Bess and Irene . . . they have a place to take you and your sisters."

"And you," Leni adds.

Yelena shakes her head.

"No." Leni shakes her head back, her lower lip trembling. "You can't go back. I don't care what Leah says about you belonging to the Red Room. You can hide from them. I know you can. You can do anything. You've pulled off every crazy thing you told me you would. You saved me and you saved my sisters and you can save yourself, Yelena. I know you can."

Yelena's throat tightens with every earnest word. She's so sure. Yelena wishes she could see the world the same way.

That heart she thought was gone—it's there in her chest, because it feels like it's breaking under Leni's faith. The same faith Yelena has to shatter.

"I can't go with you," Yelena says gently.

"They're going to hurt you if you go back, Yelena," Leni says.

"I have a plan. They're never going to know what really happened this past week."

"I didn't mean they were going to hurt you because you let us get away," Leni says. "I meant they're going to hurt you because that's what they do."

Tears sting the corners of her eyes. She has to stare up at the ceiling, trying to control herself.

"Some things," she says finally, "we must endure. So others don't have to."

Leni doesn't bother to fight the tears in her eyes. "And you have to endure, so we don't have to."

Yelena takes both her hands, squeezing them lightly. "At least I can always say: I'm worth three of you."

Leni lets out a breath that can't make it to a laugh. "I want you to come with us."

"I would if I could," Yelena says, and she finds she means it enough it's not even close to a lie.

"Am I ever going to see you again?"

"Maybe someday," Yelena says, even though she knows the answer is most likely no. It wouldn't be safe.

"It isn't fair," Leni says.

"You trust Miss Bess and Miss Irene, right?" Yelena asks.

Leni nods.

"And you kind of trust me?"

"I don't *kind of* trust you," Leni says. "I trust you. Even though it doesn't stop you from making silly decisions sometimes."

"So then I want you to do the hardest thing ever," Yelena says.

"What?" Leni asks.

"I want you to trust us," Yelena says. "Because if you do, if you let the grown-ups who love you and saved you . . . if you let them be the grown-ups, then *you* get what neither of us have gotten: You get to be the kid."

"Not the test subject," Leni says, the heaviness of her words settling between them.

"I want you to be able to be a kid," Yelena says. "One who goes to school and does homework and argues with her sisters about pizza toppings. I bet Ellie will kill—hopefully not literally—at every sport she puts her mind to. You should absolutely join the school newspaper once you're in middle school—someone needs to give you an advice column. And Leah will probably end up the star of the debate club. You can have whole lives away from all this, Leni."

"You'll be out there, stuck in it," Leni says. "It isn't fair."

"But it's my fate," Yelena says. "It's too late for me.

But I can make sure it's not too late for you, if you go with Miss Bess and Miss Irene."

"Right now?" Leni asks, her voice cracking, and it breaks Yelena. She surges forward, hugging Leni tight, pressing a kiss to the side of her head.

"Right now," Yelena says, clearing her throat, willing herself to pull away. She meets Leni's eyes with a shaky smile. "I won't forget you," she says.

"I mean, you kind of can't, unless you forget yourself," Leni says.

Yelena laughs, getting to her feet. Bess and Irene stand there, Leah and Ellie next to them.

"I wish I could know where you're going," Yelena says. "But it's better that I don't," she adds hurriedly, when Ellie opens her mouth.

"You've proved to be pretty loyal," Ellie admits grudgingly.

"High praise from you," Yelena says. "Take care of your sisters, all right? And maybe don't file down your adult teeth?"

"You can't tell me what to do," Ellie says.

"Make sure you get outside sometimes once you see a library, otherwise you might get lost in one," Yelena tells Leah, who smiles.

"Thank you for saving us," Leah says.

"Assisting in saving us," Ellie corrects.

"I was happy to assist," Yelena says. She turns back to Leni, trying to keep the smile on her face. "You'll be okay."

"But you won't be," Leni says.

Yelena leans forward, pressing a kiss to her forehead. "This is my final lesson to you, little Leni: Life is not fair. But when a good opportunity presents itself, seize the day."

"I will," Leni says. "I promise."

Yelena straightens, nodding to Bess. "Be safe. I will take care of Director Cady."

"He should be on his way here any minute now," Bess says. "Someone in town has to have spotted us and reported it to him."

"Then go quickly," Yelena says. "And don't look back."

"Thank you, Yelena," Irene says.

Yelena nods, afraid if she says anything else, she'll start to cry. She has to stay strong, so that Leni will go, so that this moment won't haunt her years down the line like it will haunt Yelena forever.

The girls file out of the diner, Leni pressing her hand against the window when she gets outside, Yelena mimicking the movement for a moment before Leni pulls away.

She waves. Yelena's fingers remain touching the glass that separates them as Leni crosses the street and gets in Irene's car.

She holds herself as still as she can as they drive away. She waits until the car turns off the street, completely out of sight, before sitting back down at the booth.

More than anything, she wants to cry. But she can't. Gone is the time for that. Gone is the girl who could do that.

She will be stone. For Leni and her sisters. She'll give them time to escape.

"You need anything else, hon?" asks the waitress.

"Yeah, can you get a fresh water?" Yelena asks. "Someone else will be joining me soon."

"Got it."

Yelena folds her hands on the table, keeping them in sight so he doesn't think she's going to shoot him.

And then she waits for Director Cady to arrive.

32.
THE MAIN STREET DINER

LOCATION: ARIZONA
OBJECTIVE: FLY TO HOME BASE

It's almost like a meditation, waiting. Yelena sits and she waits, the desert heat at her back through the diner window. She lets the sun beat on her skin, a reminder of the warmth that one little clone brought to her.

She will be cold again soon. But she wants to hold on to the memory. Who knows how long she'll get to keep it, if her plan works.

Director Cady drives up in a blacked-out SUV about an hour after Bess and Irene take Leni and her sisters away. By now, they've already boarded a private jet, on their way to an entirely new life.

Yelena can see him out the window of the diner, but she doesn't move as he stalks toward the door. There's no point in running. She won't spend her life doing it.

She may be able to outsmart Director Cady and whoever he'd send after her from the Outpost, but she knows she can't outrun the Red Room. The Commander would not rest until he found her.

She's counting on it, actually.

She remains sitting as he sweeps into the diner.

"Out!" he barks at the waitress and cook, the only two people in the restaurant. The waitress makes a noise of protest, but Yelena shakes her head at her. The woman takes the hint, fleeing with the cook.

"Where are they?" he demands.

"Gone," she says simply.

He glances down at her bracelets and then settles on a stool at the counter across from her diner booth. As if even from that distance she can't attack him at any moment and get the better of him.

At least her handlers back home understand the kind of weapons they are raising. Director Cady will never learn. His scientific impulses override sensibility and self-preservation. Yelena has to change that, and fast.

"I've got teams at each end of the street," he says. "There's no use running."

"Why are you acting like you caught me? I let myself be found."

"It was smart of you to give up," he says, folding his hands in front of him after unbuttoning his suit jacket.

"Nice black eye," Yelena says.

He flushes, his fingers coming up to touch the green-gray bruise on his cheek. "Where are they, Yelena?"

Yelena laughs. "Why would I go to all the trouble of getting the girls out of that horrible place to just give them back to you? They're gone, Director Cady. And they're going to stay gone. You're going to stop looking for them."

"Absurd," he says.

"Accurate," Yelena counters.

He shakes his head. "I assumed you had seen reason and understood you'd need them to trade for your life. But I guess I need to learn when it comes to you, you never see reason."

"Shouldn't you be glad my clones are in the wind, then?" Yelena asks. "If I am so defective, they are, too."

"Flaws can be rerouted," Director Cady says. "That was one of the points of interest of my experiment."

"And now I've gone and messed it all up," Yelena says sarcastically. "Scattered your test subjects across the globe. I've caused so much trouble. Whatever will you do?"

"I'll think of something," he says, but he sounds unsure.

"Will you?" She leans forward, taunting him. He tenses. She smiles inwardly. She just needs to lay her trap.

"Have you actually thought this through? Because unfortunately for you, I'm not one of your secret clones. I don't belong to you. I belong to someone much more *important* than you. Someone who has no idea that you've spent . . . what . . . millions of dollars on a secret cloning experiment whose end goal is to create spies so powerful that *you* will become more powerful than your superiors?"

She smiles, showing all her teeth. They're not as impressive as Ellie's terrifyingly sharp incisors, but she tries to channel her clone's unsettling energy for a moment, and the shiver that goes through Cady tells her it's working. "What do you think the Commander will say when I tell him what you've done? Because your plan to keep me locked in a bunker with my clones isn't going to happen, is it?"

"You can't manipulate me, Yelena," Director Cady says calmly.

"And you can't disappear me," Yelena says, fighting with the only weapon left: the truth. "You *have* to return me to the Red Room. You can't kill me, even if you make it look like an accident. The Commander will send people to investigate. And if you wipe my memories of this entire time, the Commander will notice. He'll already be suspicious because I missed my weekly report. If I don't make an excuse soon, he'll start to dig. He'll find out what you've been doing. There's always a paper trail when money's involved."

"I've covered my tracks," Director Cady says, but the wary thread in his voice delights her.

She's chipping away at his confidence.

"Thomas Crane—he knows about the clones, doesn't he?" Yelena asks. "The Commander will question him. He'll apply pressure. Thomas will pop like a pimple. He'll tell all your secrets."

"Then I'll kill him."

"But you can't kill me," Yelena says. "You can't make me disappear. You can't wipe my memories. And you can't replace me. Not unless you've got a sixteen-year-old version of me lying around, too."

Director Cady looks wistful, like that would be very convenient. "Alas," he says. "The three you helped escape are the only ones."

"I'm disturbed by the fact that I'm not sure if you're lying or not," Yelena says.

"I suppose you'll just have to decide to trust me, for your own peace of mind," Director Cady says with a smile. "Unless you want to drive yourself insane with a crusade. Who knows . . . maybe more do exist. You could spend your life trying to find other bunkers, other clones, other versions of you. It was most fascinating, watching how you reacted to them. I didn't expect it to drive you to these lengths."

Yelena frowns, a creeping realization skittering at the corner of her mind like a spider who's lost a leg. "Did you . . . did you do this on purpose?" she asks. "Did you make sure I was at the penthouse? Did you . . . Was this what you wanted? For me to meet Leni?"

He grins, a crazed light in his eyes that reminds her too much of the Doctor's creepy air. "It was a variable I never could have expected to bring into the experiment: contact with the Source. What would she do, when confronted with clones she didn't know existed? What would they do, when confronted with what they were taught to fear?"

"Oh my god," Yelena says. "You're sick."

"It was a spontaneous decision," he says. "But I couldn't resist. Dr. Chambers's obsession with eliminating the Heart Subject was getting truly annoying, but it presented an opportunity for you two to make contact. When the girls were given an understanding of what sisters were, fascinating changes began to occur. The experiment needed to evolve as the subjects grew, but Dr. Chambers didn't agree with me. I began to wonder how they would react to the Source. Would they see her as a sister? An enemy? Competition? Never in my wildest dreams would I have thought you would be in my grasp, but then . . . it was like the Red Room handed you to me on a silver platter. I had to see what would happen if you made contact with them."

"And are you pleased with the results?" Yelena demands, hating the way he looks at her, like he understands her more deeply than she does herself. "Have you gathered enough valuable data? Was it worth it? You've lost the clones, you've defied the Red Room—stolen from them, not just money but DNA. And if they find that out, it's all over for you. So you need to slow down and *think* for a second. About more than your experiment and about more than science. I want you to think about how to save your own skin, Director Cady. And I don't mean metaphorically. I mean they will *peel your skin off* when they find out."

He squares his shoulders like he's about to argue with her, but she surges forward, heedless of any objection. She needs to dig in the knife.

"Have you ever seen the Commander torture someone?" His eyes widen slightly. His fingers clench into fists. "Because I have," Yelena says casually, even though the memory is still seared in her brain, one of the greatest sources of her nightmares. "An enemy spy was brought in when I was fourteen. The Commander honored a few select girls by allowing them to observe. I will never forget that man's screams. How sharp a knife must be to peel skin so thin it's translucent when you hold it to the light. How I could not look away, not for one minute, because that was weakness. And I did not look away. But you, Director Cady, you are the kind of man who would. Even if it meant ruination. So I want you to consider: If you can't even stand watching it happen, how can you expect to live through such torture happening to you?"

He swallows. Sweat trickles down his temples. It's not just from the heat.

"We could make a deal," Yelena says, her voice dropping to a tempting lull. "We could spin this as a field exercise that you sent the team on. I was assigned the role of rogue agent to see how your trainees would react. The Commander would find that a reasonable explanation for why I was out of contact with Headquarters, and it would explain to my teammates why I've returned with you unpunished, if it was all a test. If they don't think it was real, then I'll be free to return home with no gossip surrounding my stay in America, to ensure that the Commander believes that while I think the trainees could improve, they have glimmers of potential. They might always be inferior compared to the girls at home, but with the right focus they can get better. And you are good at focusing girls, aren't you, Director Cady?"

"Charming, Yelena," he says. "What other lies are you planning on telling your Commander?"

"I will report that you are a distant leader but seem to be respected. But to make sure that these defects I am reporting do not fall on you, you'll let me 'discover' documentation showing that one of the Cranes drained the funds that I know *you* must have drained to provide for the clones. Thomas has a gambling problem already, after all. It'd be easy to create a paper trail of blame. The Commander will zero in on both the Cranes, and he'll likely clean house in terms of your staff, but you and the trainees will remain to rebuild."

"You've got it all planned out," Director Cady says.

"Yes, well, I learned very quickly that you are narrow-minded when it comes to plans," Yelena says. "When three eight-year-olds can outthink you, we've got a problem. You let Leah cobble together her own chemistry set with jam jars and mold or something to create her smoke bomb. Ellie *filed her teeth* so she could bite people better. Do you understand how crazy that is? And Leni! You taught Leni how to read people like a therapist. Instilling an eight-year-old with that much emotional maturity and righteousness is a recipe for moral fury. I have had to deal with *so* many lectures the last week because of your weird obsession with making my clones single-minded."

"It's why I chose you, you know," he says.

Yelena frowns. "Because of my excellent insults?"

"Your mind," he says. "Your spirit. Your strength. You embodied all three so well, I knew you were the perfect Source for the experiment. I read everything about you. All the reports. I watched all the videos of your training sessions. I even watched them strip you of your memories. You may know the screams of a man being expertly tortured, Yelena, but I know what you sound like when you scream for your mother."

The blood drains from her face as that crazed light returns to his eyes. She has to force herself to breathe normally. Giving him the pleasure of more of a reaction is exactly what he wants.

"You will take my deal," Yelena grits out. "I will return home, and you will shift blame to Thomas Crane. Problem solved."

"And why would you do this for me?" Director Cady asks. "Going to such great lengths to protect me when you could just turn me over to the Commander?"

"Because of *your* part of the agreement," Yelena says. "You'll walk away safe from this. But you'll let me walk away with what I want."

"Your life?"

"My life is not in question here. Their lives, however, are," Yelena says. "My clones. I want them safe. You won't look for them. You won't monitor them. You'll leave them be. Let them grow up. Because if you try to find them . . ."

"You'll tell the Commander?" he asks mockingly.

"No," Yelena says, because she's always one for throwing a surprise out there. "I've decided to play the long game. I'll wait until the girls are old enough. And then I'll help them get to you. Ellie would *love* to rip your face off like a drop bear."

He lets out an unconvincing chuckle. "That's a long time to wait."

"That's a long time for them to stay safe and grow strong and smart and empathetic. And for you to grow paranoid, if you never know when the consequences of your creation might be coming for you. I would always be looking over my shoulder if I were you. Or . . ." She shrugs. "We could strike a deal. We part as, well, not so much friends, but comrades in covering up the true meaning behind this mission. If one of us breaks our promises, it's destruction for both of us. So you must decide now. Do you want to spend the rest of your life running from the Red Room if I sacrifice you to them? Or do you want to continue your climb to power? Who knows, maybe you'll even succeed. Ambition can be useful fuel."

"I see you have ambition, too, Yelena," he says. "Only a canny spy would be able to play this game, let alone come up with it. If the Commander ever found out you lied this way, that you hid the existence of such a secret—"

"I am aware of the consequences," Yelena says coolly. "Which is why the Commander will never find out from me. I will keep your secrets, and you will stay away from my clones for good and never let the Red Room know they exist. Do we have a deal?"

"We have a deal."

He gets up and walks over to her, holding out his hand. She takes it and he uses the touch to yank her forward into his space. Her skin crawls at how close he is, but the creeping horror worsens as he speaks. "You should have asked for more. Demanded I never go forward with my experiments again. That I get rid of all your DNA."

Yelena shrugs, pulling away from him. "I know better than to ask for things you'll never give me. And I'm smart enough to keep an eye on you. If you do go forward, if you dare try to clone me again, you'll find yourself with a Yelena-shaped thorn in your side for the rest of your life. Every corner you turn, you'll wonder if I'm waiting behind it. Every decision that unfolds into disaster will make you wonder if I'm the engineer behind it. You'll never rise to the heights you want if you insist on drawing my attention, Director Cady. I'll make sure of it."

"But leave you and your genetic material alone and I can do as I wish?"

"It's a simple request," Yelena says. "The question is if you can stop trying to play god in the science lab and actually commit to being a leader to your students. Because that's what your girls are missing, Director

Cady. A true leader. You've been so busy trying to create the perfect warrior from science and guesswork that you neglected the homegrown girls you already have. The reason the Widows back home succeed and compete and fight to be better isn't just because we want to be the best, it's because we want to impress our leader. The first step in that is becoming a man who inspires. That would be my suggestion to you: Leave the science and test tubes behind. Look within."

"Is that what you have done, Yelena?" he asks. "Looked within?"

"I have," Yelena says. "But I found nothing but the truth that was there before: I belong to the Red Room. I was raised to become a woman who floated above the world, who saw the puppet strings most never do. I was made to help the masters who manipulated those puppet strings, and Widows are happiest doing what we were made for."

"Will you be happy?"

"If the Red Room is happy," Yelena answers.

The smile that comes across his face is terrifying. "A loyal answer from a loyal disciple."

He thinks he's one of the puppet masters.

She hopes she never has to show him that the real puppet is him.

33.
THE MAIN STREET DINER

LOCATION: ARIZONA
OBJECTIVE: SELL THE LIE

"Shall we?" Director Cady asks, gesturing toward the diner door. "I'm sure you're eager to put on a show for your teammates."

"Do you want me to take the lead or will you?" Yelena asks. Then she smirks. "I forgot: You're supposed to be showing leadership."

"Don't make me regret making an agreement with you," he warns as he touches his ear, switching on his radio. "Send in the team," he says. "Come along."

An SUV that was parked at the end of Main Street drives toward them as Director Cady opens the diner door for Yelena and she walks out onto the sidewalk.

The SUV pulls right up to the curb, almost jumping it. Yelena's not surprised to see Johanna leap out, her game face at the ready. Well. Not really at the ready, because Yelena has done a number on her face. Her right eye is so swollen it's disappeared.

"I've got restraints right here, Director Cady," Johanna says. "My team is ready."

"Yes, sir." Tiffany and Celia line up behind Johanna. "We're ready for anything."

"We won't let you down this time," Crystal pipes up. Yelena can barely see her behind the rest of them.

"Congratulations, Team Leader," Director Cady says. "Your team has passed this field exercise with flying colors."

"Great job, guys," Yelena says, pasting on a wide smile.

"Wait . . . what?" Crystal asks.

"I don't understand," Celia says. "Why isn't Yelena in handcuffs?"

"What field exercise?" Johanna asks.

"This wasn't a real mission?" Tiffany asks, incredulous. "No way. Who fakes an assassination mission?"

"Silence!" Director Cady barks. The girls snap to, lining up automatically in response to his anger.

Yelena remains where she is, waiting to take Cady's lead.

"This was indeed a training exercise disguised as a field mission," Director Cady says. "The further you get in your training, the more creative we must get. And the more we have to rely on your judgment."

"I don't get it," Crystal says. "Why isn't Yelena in handcuffs?"

"This particular exercise was designed to see if your bonds as a team are stronger than your loyalty to the Red

Room," Director Cady explains. "We wanted to know: When one of your own defects and turns traitor, what do you do?" He smiles. "I am very proud of all of you. When presented with this scenario, you all reacted with loyalty and fierceness to defeat the defector. Of course," he adds with a chuckle, "Widow Belova was merely *posing* as a traitor."

"I am so confused," Crystal says. "Yelena isn't evil? She never was?"

"This is totally messing with my mind," Tiffany says.

Johanna says nothing; she just stares at Yelena like she still wants to kill her, no matter what Director Cady says.

"Everything was fake?" Celia asks. "What about the little girl?"

"Not fake," Director Cady says. "A controlled field exercise designed to test your psychological mettle and loyalty. And you did an excellent job."

"You were in on it the whole time?" Celia asks.

"I was doing as Director Cady asked," Yelena says carefully, looking over at Celia, who doesn't look confused like the other girls. No, Celia looks like she knows Director Cady is lying. But as soon as her eyes meet Yelena's, her expression changes, her eyebrows rising in shock like her friends.

"I don't—" Johanna starts to say, but Director Cady interrupts her like he knows she's about to protest.

"Of course, it's a very good thing this *was* a field exercise and not a true field mission," he says. "As a field exercise about loyalty and how to properly react when presented with a traitorous teammate, this was a resounding success. But as an assassination mission turned hunt for a rogue agent and secondary target, your team failed terribly. At every turn, Yelena and the target evaded you and outsmarted you, even when you outnumbered her and outgunned her."

"We didn't—"

"I was not asking for objections or arguments," Director Cady says, the chill in his voice enough to make even Johanna cringe. "Be grateful I was testing the strength of your loyalty instead of the strength of your strategy. Otherwise we would be having a very different kind of conversation."

A shiver goes through all the girls—Yelena included. The menacing note in his voice would make anyone nervous, especially accompanied by that mean glint in his eye.

"Let's load up and return to headquarters," Director Cady says. "While I will not be punishing you for your lack of strategy during this exercise, I will be thinking deeply on how to train you to correct the defects this team showed during this manhunt."

"Sir, does that mean . . . Are you taking a special

interest in us?" Johanna asks. "It's just . . . you normally don't set training protocol."

"Things will be changing," Director Cady says, and Yelena tries not to feel smug that he's taking her advice about leading. "Come along, trainees. This field exercise is officially over. Time to return to the Outpost. Belova, ride with Celia. The rest of you are with me. I want a full debriefing from you on your team's thinking and strategy, Team Leader."

"Of course, sir," Johanna says, scrambling to jump ahead of the Director to open the SUV door.

Celia and Yelena load up in the back of the second SUV, tucked together as they head down Main Street.

Celia stares out the window, not saying anything, and Yelena squirms under a flash of nervousness, because it's always awkward when you're suddenly trapped in an SUV with someone who you were fighting just a day earlier. Determined not to be the one who breaks first, she stares out her window and for almost an hour, that's how it goes. Until, finally:

"I know it was a real mission." It's barely a whisper. There's no way their driver can hear it. "That little girl . . . she looked too much like you."

Yelena doesn't say anything. She keeps her eyes glued to the window, wondering how to play this.

It's all about trust, isn't it? It's a leap, no matter what.

"Did you get her out, Yelena? Is she safe?" Celia asks softly, her lips barely moving.

I don't kind of trust you. I trust you. She'll treasure those words from Leni forever, and how odd, that she never thought to hold sentences so close before.

Yelena moves her head, the barest hint of a nod.

Celia sighs in relief. She reaches out and squeezes Yelena's knee.

"It was the right thing," Celia tells her.

Yelena knows that. It's probably the last right thing she'll ever get to do.

She can picture the three of them, in a place Yelena can't know, but she can try to imagine. Somewhere safe. Somewhere that feels like a home. Somewhere the three of them can actually go from kid to teenager to adult, unburdened by experiments and training. Somewhere they can just grow up, not as weapons or tools, but as girls. As sisters.

She can see them laughing, sweet and safe. She holds it in her mind, just for a moment.

It's enough. It's *everything*.

EPILOGUE
OXFORD UNIVERSITY

LOCATION: ENGLAND
OBJECTIVE: POSE AS A SCHOLARSHIP STUDENT TO GATHER INTEL
DATE: TWO YEARS LATER

"I'll see you next class!" says Beth, the girl she always sits next to in her English Lit class.

"Bye!" Yelena waves, gathering her books and heading out of the classroom.

She's been undercover almost an entire semester now, gathering intel on a physics professor at Oxford who is on the verge of a wormhole discovery that the Red Room has been monitoring closely. Yelena has no idea why and she doesn't care. She learned, in her first year of being in the field full-time, not to ask too many questions. It's easier that way.

Her flat is close by, but the location and her desire to blend in as much as possible means she has roommates. As she climbs the narrow steps up to their flat, she can hear Lauren singing to some new Kaylie Quick song as she unlocks the door and steps inside.

"Lecture run long?" her roommate asks from the couch before she can even close the door. Yelena found her perkiness off-putting at first, but she's grown fond of Lauren. She reminds her a little bit of Celia from the Outpost. Plus, she's an endless fount of knowledge about Yelena's professor target, being a physics major.

"Had to stay behind and let Beth copy my notes," Yelena says, slumping down on the couch next to Lauren.

"A package came for you," Lauren says, tapping the brown box on the coffee table with her foot. "At least, I think it's for you. It doesn't have your name on it, but I don't know anyone in Newfoundland."

"Thanks," Yelena says, as Lauren gets up to refill her tea mug. The clink of ceramic fills the air as Yelena uses her pocketknife to break the tape on the box, pushing the flap up.

Inside the box is a folded piece of canvas, a postcard set on top. She picks up the postcard, a smile tugging at her lips as she sees the words WORLD'S BIGGEST BALL OF TWINE, along with a picture of the ball in all its glory.

She flips it over, hoping there's a message.

The handwriting isn't as childish as she expected. But Leni must be ten now. She'll be getting ready for middle school soon. Yelena wonders if she took her advice. If she's planning on joining the school paper. She hopes so.

Her fingers trace over the words. Just two sentences, but they hold a terrible temptation.

We'll be visiting Kansas the last week of August. You could seize the day.

Below the words is a sketch she is positive Leni didn't draw. It looks like Ellie's work, because it's a stick-figure Yelena being chased by a giant ball of twine, complete with a speech bubble of her screaming *Ahhh!*

Yelena stares at the postcard for a long time, thinking about the three of them in some cabin in Newfoundland, bickering about what to write down until Leni declares she'll do it herself.

She sets aside the postcard finally, picking up the canvas, unfolding the tote bag.

PROUD PARENT OF AN HONOR STUDENT
AT SMALLWOOD ELEMENTARY

Yelena laughs, especially when she sees that Leni has tied a piece of twine in a lopsided bow around one of the tote bag's handles.

"What's that?" Lauren asks, coming back from the kitchen with tea for herself and Yelena.

Yelena sets the tote bag aside.

"Just an inside joke with an old friend," she says, accepting her tea. "Tell me all about your physics class. Did Professor Ulrich say if you got the TA job with him yet?"

Lauren descends into excited chatter and Yelena tucks the postcard and tote bag away, but not before unraveling the piece of twine and wrapping it around her wrist, knotting it like a different kind of bracelet than the ones she's used to.

But it's a weapon much more powerful than any Widow's Bite.

It's a reminder:

Some puppets can cut their strings.

ACKNOWLEDGMENTS

If I used the phrase "teamwork makes the dream work" around Yelena, she'd likely find the nearest object to brain me with, but unlike spycraft, which can be a very solitary pursuit, book publishing is indeed a team sport.

Most grateful thanks must go to the amazing team behind *Secret Sisters*:

My editor, Kim Anderson, who brought this project to me to my great delight. I had such a blast working with you and developing this!

My agent, Jim McCarthy, who has helped foster so many amazing moments and connections in my book life where I get to borrow other people's worlds and characters and play with them.

Matt Taylor and Kurt Hartman who created such a beautiful cover.

The incredible team at Disney and at Marvel, whose hard work and dedication make book publishing look easy when it is anything but.

My friends at the Trifecta, who put up with my vague-posting about clones and tote bags and whatnot for quite a bit in the groupchat. Special thanks to Margaret Owen for giving me (and the world) Kaylie Quick's name.

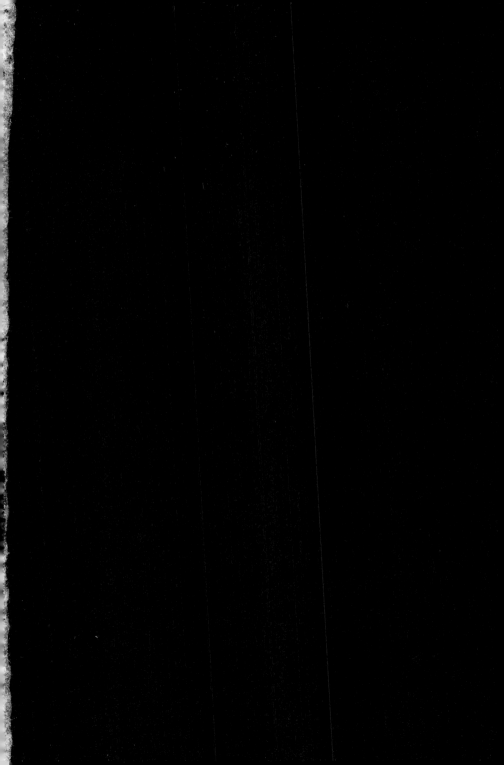